DEATH STALKS THE INNOCENTS

There was a tap at the front door. It was Symes. The expression in his dark eyes scared her.

"What do you want?" she asked, tense with apprehension.

"Love your kids?" he demanded suddenly. He took her wrist and began to twist. The pain streaked right up as far as her elbow. "Don't say a word to the police if they ask you any questions. If you do—you won't have any kids to love any more. Understand?"

She understood. She felt icy cold. No matter what she did, he was going to kill her children.

J·J·MARRIC

Gideon's Ride

ZEBRA BOOKS
KENSINGTON PUBLISHING CORP.

ZEBRA BOOKS

are published by

Kensington Publishing Corp.
475 Park Avenue South
New York, NY 10016

First Zebra Books printing: February, 1990

Printed in the United States of America

ACKNOWLEDGMENT

I would like to express my warm appreciation of the great help given me by the Press and Publications Officer, London Transport and the Superintendent, British Transport Police (London Transport) Division. They not only gave me information and advice before the book was written but read it through in manuscript and proof form, enabling me to avoid many pitfalls.

CONTENTS

Chapter		Page
1	Bus from Kilburn	11
2	The Thoughtful Criminal	19
3	V.I.P.	29
4	Kenworthy Advises	37
5	Liaison	49
6	The Kill	63
7	Failure	75
8	New Friends	91
9	New Angles	105
10	On The Run	119
11	Amok	131
12	The Other Side	141
13	Gideon Annoyed	159
14	Police Visit	173
15	Causes of Fear	181
16	Invitation to the Seaside	189
17	Strike Call	207

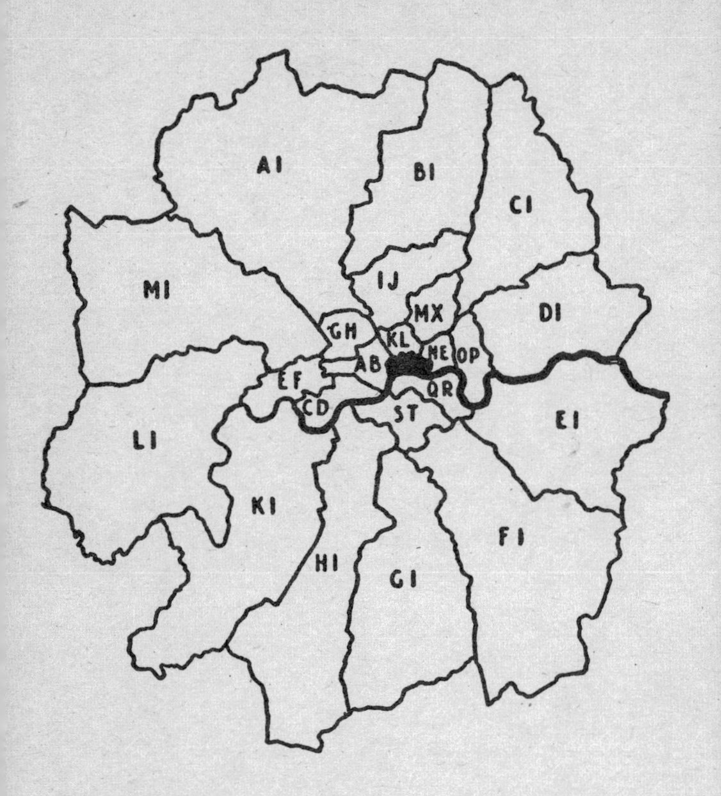

SKETCH OF GIDEON'S TERRITORY

The map conforms only approximately to the boundaries of the Metropolitan and City Police Forces, and the divisional reference letters do not coincide with the real London divisional letters or boundaries.

1

Bus From Kilburn

GIDEON liked a bus ride.

A true Londoner, one of his earliest recollections was of the thrill of clambering up the twisting, metalled stairs of the old open-type bus, and scampering along the gangway in the middle in the hope of getting a front seat, where he would have the wind cut against his eyes and face, and the whole of London stretched out in front of him. The whole of his London, that was.

Nowadays, whenever he looked at the jerky, almost comic newsreels showing the early motor buses, they seemed so top heavy it was a marvel that anyone had had the courage to mount them, let alone *run* up the stairs. He wondered what his mother, a heavy and rather cumbersome woman, must have felt when she had puffed and laboured up behind him and his brothers and sisters.

Bus rides, too, had been the joy of his own children, stretching over a period of twenty odd years. Now the last child had become so sophisticated that he regarded buses only as a necessary way of getting to a football or cricket match if the ground were too far away for comfortable cycling.

On a morning late in October, with a sharp nip in the air but bright sun over the rooftops promising a fine day, Gideon squatted on a corner of the kitchen table in his home in Hurlingham, the better residential part of Fulham, waiting for the kettle to boil before making the tea and taking it up to Kate, his wife. She was going through a tired patch, and for the past few days each member of the family had got his or her own breakfast, and Kate came down to an empty house, able to take things easy. In fact, she probably worked hard the rest of the day, but at least Gideon felt that he was doing all he reasonably could to help her. Only one boy, Malcolm, still needed much looking after. Matthew was up at Cambridge, Tom and Prudence married, the other two girls much interested in various young men.

There were times when life was almost lonely. He wondered how Kate found it.

Then he noticed a single-column newspaper headline:

MAN ROBBED ON BUS

Anything to do with crime interested Gideon, as it should interest the Commander of the Criminal Investigation Department of the Metropolitan Police. This little headline, tucked away in a corner, made him thoughtful, because there had been too many such robberies lately. A man travelling alone, on a 176 bus from Kilburn to Willesden late the night before had been set upon, beaten about the head, and robbed of all he had in his wallet—about thirty pounds. The conductress on the bus had known nothing about it until she had gone upstairs and found the injured man unconscious.

"*Humph,*" grunted Gideon, and stared out of the garden window at the dew which filmed the grass; it was already drying up in places near the house itself. Then the lid of the kettle began to dance, and he turned the gas down. The jet went too far down and went out.

Annoyed with himself, Gideon warmed the brown teapot, tossed in tea, lit the gas again, and made the tea only when the water was boiling furiously. Then he tucked the newspaper beneath his arm, and went upstairs. It was nearly nine o'clock, and only Kate was in. He had been at the Yard very late the night before, and it would not greatly matter if he did not reach his office until twelve o'clock.

He found Kate sitting up in bed, propped against the pillows, eyes laughing at him. She wore a short-sleeved, white nylon nightdress.

"Might as well kill a chap as frighten him to death," Gideon said. "How long have you been awake?"

"Ever since the kettle boiled over."

Gideon laughed. "Ears too sharp, that's your trouble. Have a good night?"

"Slept like a top." Kate hitched herself up further on the pillows. "In a day or two you might even have a wife who gets your breakfast for you."

"Never mind my breakfast, you get yourself right," ordered Gideon. He poured out, and was halfway through a cup of tea when the telephone bell rang. "Here we go," he said, half complainingly.

"What time did you get in?"

"Late-ish," replied Gideon evasively, and crossed to the other side of the bed, where the extension telephone stood. He lifted the receiver. "Gideon."

"What it is to be the boss," said a man with a twangy, Cockney voice. "Go home early, come to work late. That's my boy."

The speaker was Superintendent Lemaitre, now Gideon's second-in-command at the Yard, a kind of right arm. When he was being facetious, like this, he could be annoying, but Gideon had trained himself to think more of Lemaitre's good points than his bad: his absolute loyalty, for instance.

"What is it, Lem?"

"Nasty job on a bus last night, George."

"That Willesden job?"

"You heard about it?" Lemaitre's voice rose.

"It's in the *Express.*"

"Didn't see it there meself," complained Lemaitre. "Well, he's dead, George."

Gideon said: "Oh."

"Died without recovering consciousness," Lemaitre went on. "The conductress thinks two Teddy Boys did it. They must have given him a hell of a crack. I've been on to London Transport Police, and they're all ready for us. Anyone in particular you want to send over?"

Gideon hesitated, his thoughts running over the Superintendents who were free to take on such an investigation. He had to make sure it was someone who could work smoothly with London Transport Police, someone who really knew London, not simply a section of the metropolis. Lemaitre kept quiet; he would know instinctively what was going through Gideon's mind. Kate, sipping her tea, was watching.

"Dexter ought to be right," Gideon said at last. "Is he in yet?"

"Turned in his final report last night," answered Lemaitre. "He won't love you for it, though. He's put in for a week's leave."

"How much has he got owing?"

"Five weeks."

"He'd better have a few days off," conceded Gideon. "How about Hobbs?"

Lemaitre didn't answer.

"You there?"

"Sure. I won't run away, " said Lemaitre. "I dunno about Hobbs, though. He's a bit high-brow, isn't he? We want someone who knows his way about on buses." Lemaitre really meant that he feared that Hobbs, a public school man who had made rapid progress at the Yard through sheer intelligence, might tread on the toes of London Transport police.

"Who have you got in mind?" demanded Gideon.

"Parsons."

"He'll do," Gideon agreed at once, and wondered why he

hadn't thought of Parsons immediately. It was almost a habit to regard Parsons as a Soho and Central London man, and always a mistake. "That's if he's in."

"He got in early," said Lemaitre. "Not like some people." It was easy to imagine his grin. "Want to brief him yourself?"

"Send him over to the Willesden depot, and ask him to make sure he gets back in time to talk with me this afternoon," Gideon said. "Thanks, Lem. Anything else in?"

"Nothing that won't keep."

"I'll be in soon," Gideon said.

He replaced the reciever, and saw Kate had put a saucer over his cup. He took it off, poured in fresh tea to warm that in the cup, and sipped quickly.

"Man attacked on a bus. Died of his wounds," he told Kate briefly. "There's been too much trouble on buses lately." He smiled. "Better get it cleared up, or you'll be demanding a car."

"A car wouldn't be any good to me in London," Kate said. "Give me the bus or the tube all the time. Must you hurry off?"

"I needn't hurry, I suppose," Gideon conceded.

Nevertheless he lost no time grilling bacon and frying a couple of eggs while thinking about the dead man. All he knew, so far, was the name: Robert K. Dean. Lemaitre couldn't know much about the victim, or he would have reported.

The inevitable questions rose in Gideon's mind. How old was Dean, what kind of chap had he been, what family had he left behind, what grief and unhappiness would be caused by this? That was almost an association of ideas, and did not really concern him, although subconsciously he realized that it was his feeling for the victims of crimes which kept him on his toes so much. Being a London policeman was a vocation if one did the job well.

He did not take his car that morning, but walked to New King's Road, caught a number 22 bus as far as Harwood Road, and changed to a number 11. A front seat on the upper deck was empty. He took it, looked at the busy, familiar road ahead of him—this part of London had changed less than most—and kept hearing people behind him get on and off the bus. The man Dean must have been sitting on a bus like this, must have heard someone clatter up stairs which were so much easier to negotiate than in the old days—and then felt a blow on the back of the head.

A murderous blow, as it had turned out.

Bessie Dean could not really believe it had happened. Not to Bob. Not to *him*.

The police had been very kind and understanding, even when they had taken her to see Bob in that cold room with the hard light. Most of the newspapermen had been kind, too, although one man had kept trying to take photographs inside the house, when she had asked him not to. She had not done much about it. She had not felt that she could do much about anything. She had one heartfelt feeling of gratitude: that she had been here alone when the news had been broken.

The children were at school.

Now, with everyone gone except a single neighbour, she faced the need to tell the children, and she could not guess how it could affect either of them. How *did* a boy and girl, aged seven, face the fact that they had been orphaned? They had been so happy. Bob and her and the twins.

Quite suddenly, pain seemed to explode inside her breast, and she jumped up, her hands clenched and raised above her head.

"No, no, no!" she cried. "It can't be true, it can't be!"

She glared across at her neighbour, Mrs. Millsom, a faded middle-aged woman from next door. Mrs. Millsom was clearing the living-room table of the breakfast things. The Deans' was a small, terraced house in Willesden, not far from the depot; a house built on a site emptied by bombing. There were three bedrooms upstairs, this room, a kitchen and a small front room down here.

"Now, dear—" Mrs. Millsom began.

"I tell you it can't have happened by my Bob! God wouldn't be so cruel. It's all a mistake, it's a terrible mistake! *I couldn't have seen him.*"

"I know how you feel, dear, it must be—"

"*I tell you it couldn't have been Bob!* I've got to go to that morgue place again. It couldn't have been Bob. It must have been someone like him. I was so frightened. I didn't know what I was saying. *It couldn't have been . . .*"

She broke off, catching her breath. In that moment she realized the folly of the outburst, and the awful, inescapable fact—it had been Bob. She felt another spasm of pain in her breast, just above the heart, but did not realize its significance. Yet it was awful, it was awful. She clutched at her breast, and stared across at Mrs. Millsom, saw the alarm spring into the older woman's eyes.

"It—it hurt—it hurts so much. It—it's as if my heart's going to break," she gasped. "Oh God, the pain. Oh, the pain. Oh—"

She felt as if a knife had been thrust into her. There was another stab of excruciating pain, before everything died away except a shimmering brilliance in front of her eyes. That suddenly disappeared.

Unconscious, she fell heavily, banging her head on a chair before Mrs. Millsom could save her.

The neighbour said: "Oh, dear, what shall I do now?" She went down on her knees in front of the murdered man's wife. Worldly wise in many ways, she was perturbed by the pallor and the touch of blue at her lips. She slipped Mrs. Dean's blouse off her shoulders, hardly noticing the fine breasts, then undid the waistband of her skirt. Good gracious, she didn't wear a belt, not even a suspender belt! She had on just a flimsy brassiere, one of these half-cup things or whatever they called them, and a pair of panties. That was everything beneath the blouse and the skirt. It was almost shameful.

What a thing to think of at such a moment!

Mrs. Millsom placed a calloused hand beneath the full left

breast, and felt an unusual kind of irregular beating of the heart.

"Well, she isn't dead, that's one good thing." She hoisted herself to her feet; she was a heavy woman, and movement had never been easy for her. "I must get a doctor. Mrs. Jones will ring for one, I'm sure. I hope he's not gone out on his rounds yet. I hope—"

There was a knock at the front door.

Breathing heavily, still scared, still shocked, she padded along the narrow passage to the front door, and opened it to see three men outside. One was a policeman. One, close to the doorstep, reminded her a little vaguely of the Circuit Minister of her Methodist Church, and the third was a tall, youthful man, who stood behind the others.

"I don't know what you want, but Mrs. Dean can't see you now, she's been taken ill. She's had a seizure, I think, or a stroke. I must get a doctor."

The rather familiar-looking man answered: "Don't worry, Mrs. Millsom, I'll see that we have a doctor here at once. My name is Parsons, Superintendent Parsons of the Criminal Investigation Department." He gripped her arm, firmly. "Sergeant—telephone for a doctor at once, and make sure that he gets here quickly."

"Very good, sir," the lean young man said.

Mrs. Millsom noticed that he turned round and hurried back to the car, but did not know what he did after that. She did know that this policeman, Parsons he called himself, had a soothing effect. She was glad he was here.

That was the moment when she thought about the Dean twins.

2

The Thoughtful Criminal

AT the time when Parsons was looking into the worried face of the Deans' neighbor, when the coroner was arranging the date and time of the inquest on the murdered man, and when Gideon was at a meeting with the Commanders of the other Departments of the Metropolitan Police, a man named Kenworthy was very thoughtful indeed.

He was sitting in a café in Aldgate, the gateway to the East End of London—or, if one preferred to think of it differently, to the City of London. He was just in sight of the old pump, which had been giving water to Londoners for centuries, and now and again he glanced out of the window at the big red buses as they passed by. It was a first-floor café, and with a stretch of the imagination, Kenworthy could reach out and touch the advertisements on the sides of the buses, or the windows where the passengers sat steamed up or smoked up, looking like troglodytes.

Kenworthy believed himself to be a thinker and organizer. In fact, he was used by many of the small-time crooks who ate at the café as a grapevine.

He was known to the police, for he had once served a sentence of three months' imprisonment for picking pockets in

Petticoat Lane, and later served a sentence of six months for shop-lifting, but as far as the authorities knew, he had been clean for several years.

His wife really ran this café, and another in the Mile End Road. This one was so busy at lunch-times that only a fool could have failed to make a profit. So the police had reason to believe that Kenworthy was living fairly well, largely because of his wife's energy.

During his second period in jail, however, he had done a great deal of thinking. He had always been the ruminative type, not violent—although he had no objection to the use of violence—and not particularly original. During the second "curative" period of incarceration he had decided that he must think more about the jobs he did. There was no need to be caught, if one went about crime the right way. Since then, he had concentrated on receiving and passing on information, for a percentage. He had one or two cronies, whom he believed he organized.

He did have certain qualities and had learned a lot. He was aware, for instance, that all criminals had a kind of trade mark, and this distinguishing mark often told the police who had committed a crime. So Kenworthy changed the kinds of crime he organized, as well as the method of any crimes which he repeated. It had paid off. He was not particularly ambitious. He did not see himself as a master criminal. He was basically a lazy man, and had long believed that the clever man always got others to do the work.

He would just do the thinking.

He was in his middle forties, rather tall, black-haired, pale-faced, somewhat Italian to look at—in fact, his mother had been from Naples—with fine eyes and clearly defined eyebrows.

A few months ago, two young thieves, who lived in the dock-land area of London, had come to him in alarm. They had followed a merchant sailor, home from a long voyage, with his pockets stiff with money, caught him in a narrow street between a bus stop and Aldgate Station, where he had been heading, and attacked and robbed him. They had discovered that there was a lot of French and Dutch money among the English, and they had not known how to change it, while one of them was afraid that the sailor had recognized him.

Kenworthy had paid them half of the face value of the money, and let them work in the Mile End Road restaurant until the danger had blown over. He had never made money so easily, and the incident had started him thinking along different lines. The two youths had acted almost on impulse, but properly handled, they could pick up a lot more cash than they had from the injured sailor.

That was how Kenworthy had begun to realize the advantages of robbing individuals, usually on pay night when they were on their own. He used now ten men—the original pair and four other couples. No one pair knew of the others' existence. It wasn't exactly big business, but it brought Kenworthy in all he needed, and he was able to save a bit, too.

The man Dean had been on Kenworthy's list to be robbed for some time, because he worked a lot of overtime, and took home a big pay packet.

The *Evening News* was propped up in front of Kenworthy, and one of the double column headlines ran:

BUS MURDER—
WIDOW COLLAPSES

He knew exactly what the story said: that during the morning, after her husband had died, Mrs. Dean had suffered a heart attack and was in the hospital. Her two children, boy and girl twins, aged seven, were staying with a neighbor, a Mrs. Millsom. The grandparents lived in Devon, and the grandmother was bedridden; there would be no help from them.

Kenworthy had no feeling for the woman or for the twins, but there was another paragraph in the story which did worry him:

Conductress Helps

The conductress of the bus was able to give the police a clear description of the two men who boarded the bus in Willesden Lane and alighted at North Street, a few minutes before the injured man was found.

"So she saw them," Kenworthy muttered to himself. "Or the cops *say* she did."

He lit a cigarette, drew smoke in deeply, and let it trickle out through his nose.

His wife appeared at the kitchen doorway, glanced across and called:

"You going to stay there all day?"

"Any objection?" Kenworthy demanded.

"Only objection I've got is to you, you lazy great lout," retorted Kenworthy's wife. She moved across, rather big boned, fair-haired, smiling, wearing a grease-spotted nylon overall. "Want another cuppa, Jack?"

"Not a bad idea," said Kenworthy.

She filled a cup at a hissing, bubbling urn, then filled another, and brought them across to the table.

"I can't imagine what you sit here and think about, I really can't," she said. "If you ask me, all you do is sit and think."

"No one was asking you," he retorted. "But I'll let you into a secret."

"Okay, Jackie boy, let's have it."

"I'm thinking of how to get rich quick."

"There's one way to get rich in this world," declared his wife. "And that's to work for it. One day you'll find out, Jackie. Sooner than you expect, maybe."

He stared at her. She had a very clear complexion, in spite of the heat and the steam of the kitchen where she spent so much time. Her nose was snub. Her full lips often parted in a smile—she was a good natured, happy woman.

"What's all this?" Kenworthy demanded.

"You can think that one out," she said. "I'm not telling you. Anything in the paper?"

"Nothing much, ducks." Kenworthy pushed it across to her. As she read it, he thought of that conductress. She had seen Arty Gill and Bert Symes, who had murdered the man named Dean.

He would have to think about it. He certainly mustn't become involved in a murder charge. Arty and Bert were scared. They hadn't admitted it; in fact they had boasted of the speed with which they had done the job, and the fact that it had only taken one smack on the head from each to silence Dean, but it stood to reason—they were scared.

They were tough, he knew, but thick in the head. Before long they would come to him again; they were sure to.

Kenworthy was so preoccupied with this situation that he did not give any further thought to his wife's cryptic comment about having to work for a living sooner than he expected. She was fond of her little joke, Ivy was.

It did not occur to him to wonder what she would think if she knew that among the week's takings had been the thirty pounds stolen from the murdered man. Mixed up with all the rest of the money he had banked, there wasn't much chance that it would be identified. But he wouldn't have been so quick to pass it through to the bank if he'd known about the murder.

The situation certainly needed a lot of thinking about.

At half past five that afternoon, there was a tap at Gideon's office door. When he called "come in," Parsons entered.

No man had ever been more aptly named. He looked so like a parson when dressed in clerical grey, that to be convincing he would only have had to turn his collar round. He was a little full in the cheeks, his lips were soft looking and also full. He would purse them a lot, and would often say: *st-st-st-st* rather as if he were saying *tut-tut*. He looked a little, but only a little, unctuous. His habit of pressing the rounded tips of his fingers together was in fact part of that act in which he had trained himself. By some quirk of fate, among his early cases had been several involving vice in the West End, and today Parsons was the Yard's expert on the subject. He would talk about the most monstrous things, obscenities and indecencies, perversions and abuses, in his soft, persuasive voice, and hold an audience of hard-bitten, hard-headed policemen absolutely enthralled. It wasn't until after he had finished that one realized just how beastly the story—the factual story—had been.

He had recently been promoted to superintendency, so he could be bold.

"Hallo, Gee-Gee. How're tricks?"

"Come and sit down, Vic," Gideon said.

"Thanks. Couldn't send for a cup of tea, could you?"

"Hungry, too?"

"Parched, mostly."

"Right," said Gideon. He lifted a telephone, one of three on his desk, went on: "Messengers room," and when a messenger came on, he ordered: "Go and get some tea, for two, and bring some ham or beef sandwiches." He rang off. "Had a tough day, have you?"

"Haven't relished it much," admitted Parsons. He sat back in a green armchair which had seen a lot of use. It was in front of an empty fireplace, so that he faced Gideon. Lemaitre's chair at the littered desk, just behind him, was empty. "The doctors think Mrs. Dean will come through, but it's not certain yet. She always had a bit of a weak ticker."

"How about the two kids?"

"They're all right for the time being. Staying next door. I gather they think it's play-acting." Parsons smoothed down thinning, greying hair, and kept his hands tight on the back of his head, pulling the hair back straight, and making his forehead seem very broad and shiny. "I've checked all ways I can, George. There was nothing to it but robbery with violence."

Gideon didn't comment.

"The chap gets paid on Wednesdays," said Parsons. "Worked for a small firm of electricians. He's been on a rush job, working overtime and week-ends for the past month. That's how he came to have so much in his pocket—a week's wages plus some travelling money. Poor devil."

"Yes."

"I talked to this conductress, Winifred Wylie," Parsons went on. "Little Jamaican girl."

"Coloured?"

"Yes."

"Did she get a good sight of the two men?"

After a pause, Parsons replied: "She described them down to the colour of their socks. She keeps her eyes open all right. She says she didn't like the look of them when they got on, and they jumped off the bus without waiting for it to stop. And she says she's quite sure she would recognize 'em again. So all we've got to do is find 'em."

Gideon said: "What's gone wrong, Vic?"

"Don't know that anything has," said Parsons. "I'm just fed up with the day, that's all. I'm happier on my usual beat, George." Before Gideon could speak, Parsons went on: "I take that back. Glad of the chance of having a crack at something different. I think it was Dean's wife—the widow, I mean. I saw her just after she'd collapsed; she looked like death. This Mrs. Millsom had taken off her blouse and loosened her skirt—I suppose a copper shouldn't notice what kind of figure a woman's got, but I did. It struck me as such a bloody wicked waste. I saw the two kids when they came home from school—she never let them stay to lunch, as the school's just around the corner. Happiest pair of kids you ever saw, dressed almost identically—George!"

"Well?"

"Stop me."

"Won't do any harm to moan a bit," said Gideon. "That tea won't be long. How did you get on with the London Transport chaps?"

"All right," answered Parsons. "They're glad we're on the ball. They seem to be, too."

"How much of this robbery on buses has there been?" inquired Gideon. "Is this one of a series or an isolated instance? Any way of being sure?"

"Boman thinks we can find out, and he's as sound as they come," Parsons answered. "He says there have been a few cases, but not really a crop. Lot of minor sabotage, too, but nothing in a big way. He's digging out all the details. One robbery every two or three weeks, in different parts of London. I'll get his full report in the morning," Parsons went on. "Ah."

The door opened, and a messenger came in carrying a tray. At the same moment, one of Gideon's telephones rang. He lifted the receiver while watching the grey-haired messenger, who was working out his last months on the Force, spreading a table-napkin over a small table and smoothing it out with surprisingly frail hands.

"Gideon here."

"Information Room, Mr. Gideon," a man said briskly. "I thought you would like to know that Mrs. Dean, the widow of the man Robert Dean, died without regaining consciousness."

"Oh," said Gideon. "Bad show." He hesitated. "Thanks for telling me." He rang off, saw that Parsons was eyeing the tea as if he could not pour out quickly enough; or was he eyeing the sandwiches? They were of ham and beef, cut as Gideon liked them, with meat hanging over the sides of the thick bread.

He felt heavy-hearted; a lot of feeling had already been engendered over this murder. But there was no need to tell Parsons yet; let him enjoy his snack and relax for half an hour.

He would be told soon enough.

Gideon felt sure that this case would draw the best there was out of Parsons; thanks to Lemaitre, they had the right man for this job.

The next thing was to make sure that everyone involved handled it properly, as a good team.

3

V.I.P

AMONG the millions who read about Dean's murder and the subsequent death of Belle Dean was Sir Henry Corrington, K.C.B.E, the Deputy Chairman of the London Transport Board. Corrington had been a surprise choice for the post, and when the appointment had been announced, there had been a lot of whispering about old school tie and string pulling. In fact, Corrington had been selected because of his early training in the Diplomatic Corps—he had served both in Washington and in Moscow as a commercial attaché—and his extensive knowledge of big business.

His appointment was now a year old, and no one talked any more of undue influence. He was accepted by both management and labour, but a few knowing ones shook their heads. In the course of Corrington's year, there had been no major problems. He had not been called upon to ask the Transport Commission for an increase in fares, and none of the big unions had applied for a pay rise. The real testing time had not yet come.

"One of these days Corrington is going to run into trouble," the Jeremiahs prophesied.

Corrington lived with his wife and two daughters in a flat

near the Westminster headquarters of the Transport Commission. The daughters spent much of their time away at school. Lady Corrington, sometimes a little bored, divided her time between exclusive shops, Mayfair and Knightsbridge *salons*, and charity committees.

The Corringtons were sitting in a beautiful room, furnished in Regency style, overlooking St. James's Park. Music from a record player came softly, unobtrusive and almost melancholy chamber music with strings in the background.

Corrington put his *Evening News* down.

"I think I'll call Freddie," he said.

His wife looked up.

"What about, dear?"

"This murder."

"Oh." She frowned. "Beastly. But—" She uncrossed her slender legs. "What can Freddie do?"

"He'll know how the children are."

"He might."

"At least he'll know who does."

"I don't want to stop you," Lady Corrington said. "But don't start worrying about this too much, Harry."

"Do I worry?" He stood up, tall, lean, immaculate, distinguished-looking.

"You worry too much."

"Nonsense," murmured Corrington. "I reflect and anticipate, that's all."

He went outside and closed the door, stepped into the small book-lined library, sat at a Queen Anne desk and dialled "Freddy"—Colonel Frederick Tulson, who kept an eye on the liaison between the London Transport Police and the Yard. Tulson himself answered.

"Yes, they're being looked after," he replied. "And our man in charge, Boman—remember Boman?"

"Yes."

"He's told the neighbour who's looking after the children that we'll help where we can—meet expenses until something is sorted out, anyhow. Right?"

"Just right, Freddy."

"If you don't mind my saying so," said Tulson, "You worry about little things too much."

"So Moira tells me. Make sure the newspapers know what we're doing, won't you?" Corrington rang off, smiling faintly. As he turned round he saw his wife at the door.

"And what does Moira tell you?"

"I fuss too much over details."

"Don't you?" Moira asked.

"Depends upon how you look at it," replied Corrington. "On the principle that if you look after the pennies the pounds will look after themselves—no, I don't. If we can keep the small things running smoothly, the big ones may settle themselves. Tomorrow the newspapers will tell the world how human and considerate the Transport Commission is, acting so swiftly to help those orphans. And we will have won more goodwill."

"As well as done more good," his wife commented.

She studied him, a woman in her middle forties, nearly as tall as he, by no means a beauty but striking, with her thin features and almost teen-age figure.

"I wish you'd tell me what the trouble is."

Instead of turning the question aside by pretending that he didn't know what she was talking about, Corrington moved to her, slid an arm round her waist, and led her back to the other room. The strings still droned faintly. He went to a beautifully panelled French cabinet, and took out gin, whisky, tonic and soda-water. While each had a drink, the music faded, and the record player made a gentle clattering sound.

"My spies tell me we might run into strike trouble," he announced.

"A *strike.*"

"Startling, isn't it?"

"But everything's gone so well!"

"Too well."

"That's absurd!"

"It depends which way you look at it," Corrington replied. "There hasn't been a wage increase for a surprisingly long time. The Union's likely to ask for a big one which we can't hope to grant—"

"But darling, surely you can negotiate!"

"Oh, we'll negotiate," Corrington agreed. "But if the stories I hear are right, there's an unofficial strike committee in most of the depots, bursting for action. The Union will be reasonable, but—"

"You know, Harry, you're talking almost as if it's inevitable."

"I'm trying to think of a way of making sure it doesn't even start," Corrington told her. "Better to give it a lot of thought now, rather than wait until it's on top of us."

"I don't believe anyone who knows you even suspects how you think," Moira said. "Do you know what *I* think?"

"That I'm doddering."

"I think you're far too good for your job," said Moira. "You ought to be Minister of Transport, not—"

She broke off.

Corrington was smiling.

"It would be rather pleasant, wouldn't it?" he remarked. "But keeping on top of a section which costs seventy-five million pounds a year to operate is something in its own right."

"Seventy-five million?" Moira sounded shaken. "I'd no idea it was so much."

"Almost enough to make a profit," Corrington said lightly. "Now if we could, and if I can really find a way of cementing relations between management and labour, I'll kill the old two birds with one stone. I'd have the satisfaction of doing the job, *and* being next in line for a safe seat, and the Ministry. You know, I've always believed there must be a way to make sure of good labour relations," he added, almost dreamily. "If I could only find it—"

"You'll find it," Moira said, half laughing.

When she went to bed, half an hour or so before him, she lay thinking and wondering. Harry was an idealist, of course, and always would be, although he covered it with a veneer of cynicism. He would like the big job because of the opportunities it would give him, not simply for the prestige. She would like it for other things—its social advantages, the extra money. Whichever way one looked at it, her only course must be to help him in every way she could.

The Dean twins were fast asleep in their borrowed beds, and the Deans' house was empty and forlorn.

Parsons, a widower, read late into the night in his small West End flat, for Soho had taught him how to manage on comparatively little sleep.

Kenworthy's last thoughts, before dropping off, were that he would have to watch things. His wife slept the silent deep sleep of the physically exhausted.

Little Winifred Wylie could not get to sleep. Whenever she closed her eyes, she saw a picture of the man lolling back in his seat, blood dripping from his head; and then she would see the faces of the two youths who had gone upstairs quietly and soon come clattering down to jump off the bus. At the time, she hadn't liked them—just the sight of them had frightened her, she couldn't think why, at the time.

Art Gill and Bert Symes slept soundly enough, each in a small room in his parents' East End home. None of the parents had the faintest idea that the boys were criminals.

Gideon slept well, too, although he woke soon after six o'clock, and lay on his side facing the door wall for some time. Then he eased his big body over cautiously, so as not to disturb Kate. She was lying with her head low on the pillows, but her mouth clear of the clothes. He found himself thinking of those orphaned twins, and the biting irony of the fact that somewhere in London, perhaps very close by, the killers were sleeping, too—the murder money probably spent by now.

He began to think about the problems of the buses and of London Transport generally. Criminals on the Underground itself, and on London Transport property, like the vandals who committed minor acts of sabotage, the pick-pockets, the bag-snatching, the short-changing, were all handled by the Transport men, who knew their job inside out. Only when it came to crimes on the buses on London's highways did the Metropolitan Police take over.

Although Colonel Frederick Tulson would never admit it, T.P., as the Yard called the Transport force, was very much like one of the provincial forces, handling the crime in its own manor, and asking for help only in the acute or intractable problems, when it called in the Yard. There was the fullest co-operation, and Gideon studied the Transport reports and criminal statistics regularly, so as to get a detailed picture. He needed such a picture in order to have a complete grasp of the London crime situation. It would be easy to look as if he were poking his nose in, however, and a case like this gave him a chance of seeing the position at close quarters, without treading on any toes.

He got up, without disturbing Kate, put on a dressing-gown, and went along to the bathroom. It was a duller morning than yesterday, without any promise of sun; rain was more likely. None of the rest of the family was up. He closed the door and ran the bath, got in and soaked himself. Head and the tips of his toes above water in the pale green bath, he let thoughts drift.

It was an "off" period at the Yard. An exceptionally warm early summer followed by a thundery period and added to the light evenings and short working hours for night criminals, had given the Yard more leisure than it had known for years. Even wage snatches had been few in number. Some of the Yard's top men regarded this as an indication that the crime graph had reached its peak, and was falling. The next three months should tell. Whatever the reasons, Gideon's own desk was comparatively clear.

If he decided to take a closer look at the Transport Police and its problems, there would be no practical obstacle.

He smiled wryly to himself, and started to get up, almost elephantine until he was on his feet.

"Wouldn't be surprised if I walk into a packet of trouble at the office now," he confided to the gurgling waste, as he towelled himself. "Just the kind of thing that would happen."

The morning rush hour on both bus and Underground was still an hour away. He had a feeling that he would like to be in it. A restless mood, sparked by the bus murder, but not by any means unusual. One of the troubles with being at the Yard, involved in never-ending conferences, the continual survey of investigations and the giving of instructions, was to make him remote from the life of the city, the people and their daily grind. He ought to be out and about more, to feel the pulse of London's millions. And he must travel more by bus and tube!

He stepped out of the house eagerly.

The freshly made-up girls in the light summer dresses which emphasized their provocative little bodies, the rather earnest young men, the curious sense of controlled haste, a kind of repressed urgency among the older people; the masses of people at the big junctions; the resigned patience of the ticket collectors and the conductors and conductresses—all of these things struck him with fresh vividness. He was tempted to go out to Willesden and catch a 176 bus, but decided against it: he might bump into Parsons. He noticed a little coloured conductress of a Number 11 bus working away at her ticket machine. She had a smile for everyone.

What kind of woman was the other conductress—Winifred Wylie?

Bright, merry, smiling? Or one of the Jamaicans who found life difficult over here?

A few miles away, Arty Gill was still lying in bed, but he

had been awake for some time. He kept thinking of the black girl, the clippie. She had seen him very clearly, and wasn't likely to forget his face. That meant she would always be dangerous—to Bert as well as to himself.

He would have to decide what to do about her, soon. He would have to get to work on Kenworthy, too.

4

Kenworthy Advises

"WELL, what do you want to do?" asked Kenworthy.

"What do *you* think?" countered Arty Gill.

"You tell me," Kenworthy said.

He sat at the wheel of his dark blue Ford Consul, turning round in his seat to look at Arty. They were parked at Tower Hill, as good a place to meet as any, because there were always so many people about, so many tourists and school kids, and the police took no special notice of anyone.

Arty was rather short, thin and wiry. His hair was fair, not quite yellow and not quite ginger—marmalade, according to his current girl friend. He had greeny-grey eyes. There was something about the thinness of his lips, especially the tightness at the corners, which would have made some intelligent people suspicious of him—just a little uncertain what qualities of evil might lie behind that rather high forehead. He wasn't bad looking, but his one real grudge against life was that he had so many freckles.

Looking at him, Kenworthy realized for the first time that Arty Gill would be a very easy man to remember and to describe.

Kenworthy felt a quiver of uneasiness.

"Listen, Ken old boy," Arty said, with his assumption of equality which always riled Kenworthy, "you've just got to look at the facts. That little black tart saw me, didn't she? If they ever put me up in front of her, she'll know me. Don't make any mistake about that—they don't miss anything, these niggers."

"So she can recognize you."

"So she can send me down for a long stretch."

"Maybe," Kenworthy said.

Arty moistened his lips. His tongue was very red, curiously like an animal's. His eyes were narrowed, now, as if there was something he did not understand, and did not like. He had a half-smoked cigarette in his hand; he put it to his lips and drew slowly.

"What's got into you?" he demanded. "What's the matter with you?"

"I'm all right," Kenworthy said. "I'm just thinking."

"This time, we need *action.*"

"We want to be careful about what action we take," said Kenworthy. He ignored an impatient gesture from the youth, and went on: "You had too much action the day before last. If you hadn't killed that chap there wouldn't have been any trouble."

"Listen, Ken—"

"Now you listen to me," Kenworthy interrupted roughly. "And don't give me so much of your damned lip. You killed this guy. *You* killed him—got that? You and Bert between you. For that you could get a lifer. I don't know if they could hang you or not, maybe they couldn't, but you would certainly get a lifer."

Arty Gill muttered: "Don't rub it in."

"So long as you realize what you've done, you nit. You've got yourself in real trouble and you want me to get you out of it."

"Ken—"

"Shut up! How can I think if you keep interrupting?" Kenworthy was trying to force his mind to work as quickly as his tongue wanted to wag. "You want to croak this clippie, because she's the only one who can identify you. That right?"

"You know it is," Gill muttered.

"You *sure* no one else saw you?"

"I'm sure."

"What about the bus driver?"

"He wasn't ever close enough to get a good look. It was dark, remember. It was only when we got on the bus that there was enough light for anyone to see us."

"Any other passengers?"

"Listen, I've told you—"

"Well, tell me again," said Kenworthy. Arty must be kept in his place. "Were there any other passengers?"

"There were a few inside, but—"

"How many is a few?"

"I dunno. Three or four, maybe half a dozen, but they didn't see me."

"How do you know they didn't?"

"They all had their backs to us."

"Sure?"

"For God's sake!" Arty Gill almost shrieked, "what's going on? I tell you they all had their backs to us!"

"What about the side seats, near the platform?"

"They were empty."

"If you're sure they were empty—"

"I'm telling you, aren't I?"

"Pipe down," Kenworthy snapped. "You'll have half the beefeaters staring at us in a minute." In fact, the custodians of the Tower were out of sight, down by the entrance. Nearby, surrounded by a group of American tourists, one of the guards marched to and fro, rifle at the slope. "So no one else could have had a good look at you, and this Jamaican clippie is the only one who could identify you," Kenworthy went on. "That's a fact."

"I've been telling you it is." Arty was sweating, and there was a scared and yet angry look in his eyes. "Listen, all you've got to do is find out who she is. Just find out who she is, and leave the rest to me. I don't want you to get your fingers dirty, you needn't worry about that."

"*I'm* not going to kill anyone."

"But I've got to get rid of her—even you can see that?"

"Yes," said Kenworthy slowly. "I can see that's what you'd rather do than spend the next twenty years inside. Listen, Arty, I'm not promising anything, but I'll try to find out where she lives. I've got pals in Willesden, they can get busy. If I can put a finger on her, then it's up to you."

"You needn't worry about that. I'll fix it."

"Yes," said Kenworthy, slowly. "Yes, I believe you will. Okay, scram. Tell Bert I want him."

"You fix this and you won't ever regret it." Gill's eyes were very bright.

"Don't you worry, I'll fix it."

Arty gripped his hand tightly, then opened the door—and a car horn honked an urgent warning. A taxi swept past, within hand's reach. The driver glared. Arty licked his lips, glanced out this time, and then got out. He was wiping his forehead when he walked across the cobbles towards a coffee stall where Bert Symes was having a cup of tea and a sandwich.

Bert was short, thickset and dark-haired. He walked towards the car with a curiously jerky motion, feet splaying a little. He got in beside Kenworthy, and wiped some crumbs off his mouth. He needed a shave. He had small, deep set, very dark-blue eyes which kept very steady and seldom avoided the direct glance.

"Want me, Ken?"

"Just answer some questions, will you?" Kenworthy asked, and proceeded to put exactly the same questions as he had to Gill. All the answers were the same. There was no emotion, no hint of fright or nervousness, in Symes's manner—rather something hard and rock-like.

"So if this coloured clippie fades away, no one can fix you or Arty," Kenworthy remarked.

"Right."

"You talked to Arty about it?"

"You bet I have."

"You really thought about it?"

"Don't you do the thinking around here?" It was difficult to be sure whether there was any sarcasm in that remark.

"Supposing you bump off the clippie—everyone will know why. It's bad enough now, there'll be plenty big hunt for you, but if the clippie dies, the police will hot up the pace."

"Will that matter, if no one sees us?"

"How are you going to make sure no one sees you when you fix her?"

"I'll make sure," Symes said.

"How can you?"

"You've got to leave some things to me," declared Symes. "You've got to trust me. And don't try to pull a fast one over me, Ken. If the police pick up Arty, he'll talk. They wouldn't get anything out of me, but Arty will talk—and that will bring you into it. Don't forget you're an accessory after the fact, and seeing the way you've been earning a living lately, that wouldn't go down so well in court."

Kenworthy said, almost unbelievingly: "Are you threatening *me?*"

"I'm just pointing out the facts," retorted Symes. "I'm just telling you that if that clippie identifies me or Art, you'll be brought bang into it. It's as important to you as it is to us to fix that conductress. I just want you to be sure."

"You've made yourself clear," Kenworthy said, in a taut voice.

"That was the idea."

Kenworthy spoke very slowly and carefully.

"You and Arty can get yourselves lost for a day or so," he

said. "Keep under cover—I'll fix a job at a garage. That description could be fastened on to Arty easily. There are plenty of others it would fit, but it might be put straight on to Arty. So keep out of sight. As soon as I know where to find that clippie, I'll tell you. And then it will be up to you."

"Right," said Symes. "That's the lot?"

"Isn't it enough?"

"So long as we understand each other," Symes said.

He twisted round in his seat, looked out of the window and made sure that nothing was coming, got out, bent down as he slammed the door and gave a mock salute, then turned and marched briskly back towards the coffee stall. He did not look back. Kenworthy stared at him until only the bottom of his coat, his legs and those splay feet were visible above the window frame. Soon, he moved off down the hill—on his own. Several minutes later, Arty went in the same direction.

Kenworthy had always known that Symes was the stronger character of the two, although in the past he had said little, and Arty had appeared to be the leader. There was now no question about Symes. He had character and quality and ability, and brains, although he wasn't yet twenty. A man like Symes could go a long way, properly handled. The important thing was that he should not realize that he was being handled.

Kenworthy started the car, let in the clutch, and eased out of the parking place. Soon, he was heading for Aldgate, and pondering the best way to get out to Willesden. Commercial Road, City Road, Pentonville—yes, that was it. Out to Hampstead that way, and cut across. It would save a lot of traffic. He had to do it in person, it was no use telephoning. With luck he would be able to find out the address of this conductress without anyone knowing. With luck? A man had to make his own luck. He mustn't take any chance of being connected with the girl now—he had to think his way round this one.

But on the whole, he was not unhappy. His high opinion of

himself remained.

It was not, after all, a heavy morning at the Yard.

Lemaitre was in, sitting in his shirt-sleeves. His shirt was television white, and this morning his blue and white spotted tie was more subdued than usual. He wore a blue suit, the jacket hanging neatly on a hanger on the stand by the door. Some years ago, Lemaitre had gone through a very rough period, and his first marriage had broken up. Few things had more pleased Gideon, for the first Mrs. Lemaitre had been an out-and-out bitch. But Lemaitre had found bachelor life wearisome, and after two years of it he had married a pleasant, hearty, extremely capable woman fifteen years his junior. She liked her Lem to be smart, and even liked his choice of clothes and colours, but made quite sure that he was always turned out like a new pin.

"Morning, George." He put down a pencil and pushed his chair back. "Been a fairly quiet night. Couple of burglaries over at Chelsea, looks as if they're the same man. Post Office job at Kensal Rise, but they didn't get away with much. Woman's body found cut up in Frith Street, nasty business—Parsons' line, usually, but I didn't think you would want to take him off the Dean case, so who do you think I sent?"

Lemaitre was grinning broadly.

Gideon took off his coat and draped it over the back of his chair.

"Hobbs," he guessed.

"Think you're smart, don't you? Yes—he's on the job already. Bit beneath him, doncher know, but—"

"Stop taking a rise out of Hobbs," said Gideon. "He's going to be sitting in this office one of these days."

"That'll be known as Crooks' Celebration Day, that will."

Gideon laughed. "What else is there?"

"They picked up the Swiss who was bringing in industrial

diamonds—had 'em packed inside some cigarettes. You'd think they would think up something new sometimes, wouldn't you?" He grinned. "Seven year old girl missing, up near Newcastle. They think they know who snatched her, and don't intend to ask for any help just yet. Manchester's found those two who escaped from Strangeways." Lemaitre was turning over pages of a report which was written in his small, very neat handwriting; almost miniature copperplate. "There are four in the queue for you this morning, and I put Parsons last—thought you'd need more time for him."

"I shall," said Gideon. "Thanks."

He sat down, sifted through some papers, and noticed a request from the Assistant Commissioner, Lt. Colonel Rogerson, to go and see him at 10:30. There was no indication as to the reason, so it would probably be administrative. Gideon put the files aside, and looked across at Lemaitre.

"Ready?" Lemaitre asked.

"Bring 'em in."

It was the usual morning briefing, and on occasions Gideon would have as many as twenty senior officers to see. Each would tell him how the investigation he was handling was going; Gideon would make suggestions, indicate possibilities, and ponder the case during the day, to see if he could pick up an angle not yet seen. While he often deplored the fact that he had to sit here so much, he knew that by sitting at this big flat-topped desk he could be more objective. His vision not obscured by the immediate problems of a case.

Riddell, now one of the senior superintendents, came to report on a robbery with violence investigation now three weeks old. He had not got much farther, and seemed disappointed when Gideon could make no new suggestions. Gideon arranged to see him again, later in the week, then spent ten minutes with a younger man with a disconcertingly similar name—Ringall.

Ringall, big, bluff, typical of the stage detective, had a

remarkable memory and a grasp of detail, but Gideon did not think he had ever had an original idea. He was busy working on the Seaside Murders—the murders of three girls in their teens, one at Brighton, one at Bournemouth, one at Southend, over a period of four months. There had been marked similarities. Each girl had been either raped or seduced—more likely seduced, since there had been little sign of a struggle—and strangled. The crimes had been committed at intervals of several weeks, and there was no certainty that they had been committed by the same man.

"How's it going, Ring?" Gideon asked.

"As a matter of fact, I might have had a break," Ringall said. He was very red in the face, one of those men who never really took sunburn well, although he was not likely to blister. He had pale brown eyes and colourless lashes and eyebrows. "You remember that London bus ticket we found on the Brighton job—Number 15 bus, for a journey between Marble Arch and Paddington?"

Gideon thought: *Bus* ticket.

"Yes."

"Well, another Number 15 ticket's turned up at Bournemouth. Someone had screwed up half a dozen tickets and an old envelope, and thrown 'em away. You know how you empty your pockets of rubbish sometimes. Looks as if this chap did that."

"Any name on the envelope?"

"No, worse luck—a window envelope, you can buy 'em anywhere. We can't prove it's connected with the murder there, but it's an interesting coincidence. It was found in a waste-paper basket in a car park near the murder spot—Alum Chine. The other one was found in a waste-paper basket near a car park in Brighton, near *that* murder spot."

Gideon nodded.

"Bournemouth's doing a print search on this one. They'll get something off the envelope for sure. We had a fragment of a print on that Brighton ticket. If we find another on this one, and it turns out to be the same—"

"When's Bournemouth sending the report up?"

"It'll be on the ten-forty from Bournemouth Central. I'm having a man take it off the train at a quarter to one. Should know for certain this afternoon. Gave me quite a lift," went on Ringall.

He really meant that he was delighted with himself for arranging to have the waste-paper basket search, and was asking for a pat on the back.

"Be a putty medal for you if we can trace him," Gideon said, and won the expected flush of pleasure. "Funny thing, a bus ticket."

"Funny?"

"The Dean job."

"Oh, yes, that," said Ringall. "Can't say I'd seen the connection until you mentioned it. Well, I'll keep in touch. Be here this afternoon, won't you?"

"Yes."

"Good. See you." Ringall raised a hand to Lemaitre, who flicked a finger at him, and went out. The door closed with a hiss of the hydraulic self-closer.

Lemaitre raised his eyes ceilingwards.

"We do get 'em, George, don't we? I've got good news for you. Harrison's cried off—he won't be seeing you this morning. He's had a squeal from Division and thinks he ought to check it right away. Parsons was called out, too—said he'd give you a buzz."

"He wouldn't go off unless it was urgent," remarked Gideon. "Wonder if he's got anything. Anything else in?"

"Nothing fresh."

"You know the trouble, don't you?" said Gideon. "You haven't got enough to do. Go through our records for crimes on buses and trains in the London Transport area for the past year, will you? Get a summary out, as far as it can be done."

"What's on your mind now?" demanded Lemaitre.

"If I'm going to have to talk to the T.P. chaps I'd better seem to know what I'm talking about," said Gideon. "It's ten past ten. I'm going down to Information for a word with Hebb, and then I'm going along to see the A.C. Hold everything, unless it's urgent."

5

Liason

ROGERSON and Gideon had worked together for a long time, Rogerson mostly on the administrative side of the Criminal Investigation Department. He was a retired regular Army man—Coldstream Guards—and for some years had been very careful because of a heart which had once nearly faded out on him. His lips had the slightly blue tinge of the heart case, and whenever he exerted himself, he breathed heavily, and was liable to have palpitations. There were some who said that he should have retired by now, and that Gideon should be in his place. Gideon was more than content with the Commander's job, at least for the time being. At fifty-three there was still plenty of time, and an Assistant Commissioner was even further removed from the rank and file, and from the real life and crime of London.

Rogerson had become rather plump, and a little careless about his hair. Now, it needed cutting; another time, it might be almost cropped.

"Come in, George." He pointed to a chair. "Bit stuffy this morning, isn't it?"

"It'll turn to thunder," Gideon prophesied as he lowered himself into a big armchair. He waited for Rogerson, making no attempt to guess what this was all about.

"Dare say," said Rogerson. "George, I had a funny kind of talk this morning, with Tulson. You know, Colonel Tulson of the Transport Board."

"I know."

"He started in about the bus murder, and then rambled a bit, but he's not a rambler by nature," Rogerson went on. "He was getting at something."

Gideon waited.

"Wanted to know how the liaison is working out between us and his chaps over this investigation." Rogerson rubbed the tip of his nose. "He seemed anxious to make sure that we haven't spotted anything his chaps have missed."

"We haven't, yet."

"That'll please him," said Rogerson. "Tulson said he'd like you to have a word with Boman on the murder job, and not leave the liaison entirely between Boman and Parsons."

"Are they clashing?"

"He was at pains to say they weren't, but I wouldn't like to be sure. Hearing Tulson humming and hah-ing is like hearing a Rolls missing on two or three cylinders. Could be he feels we ought to have a V.I.P. on the case. Fix up to see Boman today if you can."

"I will," promised Gideon. He put his hand inside his jacket pocket and smoothed the bowl of the big pipe which he always carried there, but seldom smoked. It was a kind of good luck charm—or talisman, and also a kind of comforter. When really puzzled he would often smooth it, as he was doing now, and poke the tops of his fingers into the big bowl; there was barely room for the middle finger, but all the rest went in easily. "Funny thing, but Parsons was coming to see me, and cried off. Could there be a connection?"

"Leave it to you to find out," Rogerson said. "I gather things are fairly quiet."

"Not bad," said Gideon. "Don't run away with the idea that we can spare any staff if T.P.'s short-handed, though."

"Good old George," said Rogerson, and gave a deep chuckle. "Fight to the death to keep the Department at strength, won't you?"

"Don't make any mistake about this," Gideon said soberly. "If half a dozen big crimes came, all of a sudden, we would be stretched so tight, finding the right men to handle them, that something would crack. I'm just keeping my fingers crossed until the holiday season's over."

When he got back to his office, he decided that he would wait until Parsons got in touch with him; it would be much better if the next move came from the man on the job.

Lemaitre was speaking into the phone. Gideon recalled what Rogerson had said, and grinned at himself.

Lemaitre put his left hand over the mouthpiece.

"All right for Parsons and Boman at three o'clock, George?"

"Suits me," agreed Gideon, and glanced down at his desk. On top of it were the latest details of the evening papers. One of these had a headline right across the page, the other a deeper but narrow one.

LONDON TRANSPORT BOARD TO AID ORPHANS

TRANSPORT EXECUTIVE COMMISSION AIDS MURDER TWINS

"H'm," muttered Gideon.

"Say something?" Lemaitre inquired.

"Must have a good Press Officer," Gideon said, reading the story.

"Struck lucky, that's all," opined Lemaitre. "The papers are always scratching around for news in the summer—if there isn't a Test Match or Wimbledon or—" He broke off as the telephone bell rang, and he lifted the receiver quickly: "Lemaitre. Yes, I'll hold on." He covered the mouthpiece again and flexed his fingers around it. "Bournemouth," he whispered. "That reminds me, George—we haven't laid anything on for the Oval Test Match."

"Routine," said Gideon.

"No changes?"

Gideon said: "I don't see any need—" and broke off. "Wait a minute, though." One of the problems of the great sporting occasions was transport. The bus service and the Underground services would be stretched to their uttermost, and it might be a subject to bring up to Boman. The C.I.D. as well as the London Transport police watched the buses and the crowds, on the look-out for pick-pockets.

Lemaitre's eyes lit up.

"Yep, speaking . . . Hi, Tom, what's it like down at the briny? . . . I bet you're sunburned down as far as your naval. What's all this about . . . Eh? . . . Sure? Well, that's a bit of all right. Yes, I'll tell him. Love to Mary."

Lemaitre rang off, cocked a thumb at Gideon, made a note, and then said:

"They found a fragment of a print on that bus ticket Ringall was so bucked about, and a full print on the envelope the tickets were screwed up in."

"That's all?"

"Corblimey, how much more do you want? No, there's plenty more. The print is identical with one they found on the locket that girl had round her neck. Ringall's really on to something, George. He'll be like a dog with two tails and a pair of . . ."

"Where is he?" demanded Gideon.

"In his office, I think—unless he's gone over to Waterloo to pick up the ticket off the train."

"He wouldn't do that," said Gideon. "Give him a call, and tell him the good news."

He sat back, glancing through the newspaper story of the gesture by the London Transport Board over the two children. It was a very good one, and would make a hit with a lot of people. He wondered whose idea it was, and that carried his thoughts to Tulson's "odd conversation". Was that part of the same situation? He did not give it too much thought, and had time to feel a glow of real satisfaction that there were signs of getting nearer the end of the three girl-murder cases. Seaside jobs, with a shifting population such as all the resorts had, were the very devil. Two bus tickets thrown away by a man with an anti-litter attitude. Odd, how things worked out. They might go six years without a bus ticket being a clue in a murder job.

A photograph at the foot of the front page of the *Evening News* caught his eye. It was of a colored woman bus conductress, wearing her leather straps and ticket machine, and also a peaked cap. She looked small and thin, and there seemed to be something nervous about her, although her smile was bright enough. The caption read:

Winifred Wylie—the Conductress who found the body.

There was nothing else; no interview with the woman was reported, nothing more was said to tie her up with the Dean murder and the death of Mrs. Dean. Gideon let his thoughts run on again. Her name had been kept out of the early publicity because of a request by the London Transport Police. Was it just possible that she knew anything about the crime? Could she have been an accomplice in any way at all? Could she have tipped off the killers, for instance, so that they had known that Dean was on the top deck, alone? He might be stretching his imagination too far, but Parsons hadn't suggested this and it was surely worthwhile looking into it—*all* possibilities were.

It was a good picture, as Press pictures went. Very good. No one could possibly have any difficulty in recognizing her.

Kenworthy was the first of the three men concerned to see the photograph.

He was at Willesden, having a steak pie and mashed potatoes at a small café near the bus garage, knowing that a lot of drivers and conductors and other Transport workers would patronize it. He bought a newspaper to glance at and so hide the fact that he was looking round, saw the big headline and screwed up his nose—and saw the photograph. His eyes widened, and for a moment he held his breath.

"*Winifred Wylie,*" he whispered to himself.

A man sitting at a small, formica topped table near him, looked up.

"Very nice gesture, your people have made," Kenworthy remarked.

"My what?"

"Your people."

"Who'd you mean, my people?" The other man was big, gruff, blue-jowled.

"London Transport. That's you, isn't it?"

"Bloody bosses—screw us workers down to the last penny but give the money away when the Government ought to do it." The man looked down at his plate, gripping his knife and fork as if he wished they were bludgeons.

Kenworthy noticed several other men glance across, one grinning, one frowning, most with outward indifference. He wished he had not drawn attention to himself, and disliked the big man with sharp intensity. The man soon left, and another, younger, thinner man shifted his position and sat next to Kenworthy.

"Don't take any notice of him, mate. He's a blinkin' Commie. Nothing's good enough for him."

"I didn't mean to cause any offense," Kenworthy said, stiffly.

"He shouldn't have taken none, neither. Not often the old L.T.B. shows a bit of heart." He spoke with a kind of affection which would undoubtedly have done Corrington good to hear. "But it's not so bad, I've worked on the buses for twenty years. Could do with another quid a week, but me missus goes out to work a coupla mornings, and the kids are O.K. at school. We're all right."

"That's good," said Kenworthy. "Terrible thing to happen, wasn't it?"

"Bit of a bleeder," the friendly man remarked. "You get

some queer types on the buses, especially late at night. Drunks and couples, they're the trouble. Do you know, a week or so ago I went up to change the sign at the front and there was a couple up to it on the seats. Blinkin' miracle it was. Not much more than kids, anyhow."

"Have you ever had any trouble?" Kenworthy inquired.

"Not to say trouble. Caught an old man with his hand inside a woman's handbag once."

"Better than inside her blouse. Think women conductresses ought to do the late turns?"

"No reason why not. They've got the vote, haven't they? Always talking about equality. Just bad luck on Winnie, that's what it was."

"Winnie?" Kenworthy's heart began to thump.

"You know, the conductress on that 176. Winnie Wylie. Decent kid too—'ad a bit of bad luck before that."

"What kind of bad luck?"

The busman sniffed.

"Husband walked out on her—for a *white* girl, believe it or not."

"What a shame," Kenworthy made himself say.

"Shame's the word all right, mate. So she's on her own. Leaves her kid with the landlady while she works. She doesn't often work late shift, but it's the holidays."

Kenworthy dared a direct question.

"They've given her a rest, I suppose?"

"Offered it to her, but she wouldn't take it," the garrulous man said. "She's got what it takes, Winnie has. She'll be in soon for a cuppa before she starts her shift. And it's time I got a move on, mate—if I miss my turn I'll be in the dirt. So long."

He went off, paid his bill at the cash desk near the door, and went out. Several others followed, leaving the café nearly empty. Kenworthy ordered a piece of jam roll and a cup of coffee. As he turned away from the counter with the coffee, the door opened and Winifred Wylie came in, followed by an elderly, hard-faced man also in uniform.

Men and woman called out.

"Hi Winnie!"

"How're tricks, Win?"

"Look after her, Dave."

Kenworthy was quite oblivious of the tone of sympathetic warmth in the voices. He had one good look at the conductress, and knew exactly what Arty and Bert meant. Winifred Wylie had fine, glowing black eyes, eyes which seemed to see deeply and vividly. Her gaze rested only for a moment on Kenworthy but it made him feel uneasy. She had a clear, shiny complexion and was darker than the photograph had indicated. Her smile for those who greeted her was quick and warm.

Kenworthy drank his coffee quickly, and left.

He drove straight back to the Aldgate café, where Ivy was helping with the washing up. He wasn't surprised to see Arty Gill at a table, facing the window with a copy of the *Evening News* propped up in front of him. Arty's eyes had an unnatural brightness, and he kept snapping his fingers.

"You seen this?" he demanded.

"Have I seen what?"

"You know. This picture."

"I've seen more than that—I've seen the original."

"In *person?*"

"In the flesh."

"Listen, Ken, is she—"

"She's on duty," Kenworthy said. "She'll be on the Number 176 route again today. If you want a chance, you've got it."

"Do I want a chance!" Arty said, thickly.

"Where's Bert?"

"He's at the garage."

"Tell him what I've told you."

"I can't wait."

"Listen, Arty," Kenworthy said, and leaned forward, hands resting heavily on the desk. "You messed things up the night before last. Don't do it again. Understand? Make a good clean job. We don't want any more trouble."

"There won't be any more trouble," Arty assured him. "I'll be at the bus garage, and follow her home. We'll get her on the way."

"So long as you do," Kenworthy said.

Driving Ivy to the small flat which he rented on a London County Council Estate near Whitechapel, he felt strangely uneasy. He had never seen himself as a murderer—well, anyhow, *he* wasn't a murderer, was he? He had never expected to become involved in anything like this, but it was the only safe thing to do.

That damned woman's eyes seemed to follow him everywhere he went.

Ivy seemed too tired to notice that he was preoccupied; for once she didn't tease him. That was as well, for he had never felt less like being teased.

He got home with her at four o'clock.

Among the men who had heard the burly busman talk to Kenworthy were old Joe Ware and Fred Dibben.

"Old" was nearly right, for Joe was over sixty, and not very far off retirement. He was one of the best known men on London's bus transport service, he had worked on it since the age of twelve. He had started as a cleaner's help, sweeping up and tidying in the depots, then a cleaner proper, and had dreamed of becoming a conductor. The decimation of male workers in the First World War had given him his chance much earlier than he had expected, and he had been made a conductor at the age of seventeen, on the London General Omnibus Company.

In those days there had still been some horse-drawn omnibuses.

One of his drivers, in those early, youthful days, had gone to visit his parents, and in the cellar of an old house in East Ham, had discovered a working model of the London General tours made with almost unbelievable care and precision by Joe, with some help from his crippled father. The driver had talked about this so much that dozens of visitors had gone to see the model. Gradually, Joe's hopes, ambitions and objectives had increased. He set out to make an absolutely perfect scale model, including buses, horses, depots; but soon he had come up against the obvious problem—lack of space.

Still, he dreamed.

Not far away as the crow flies, although a long and devious way by bus or even Underground, there had lived another enthusiast for London and London's transport—Fred Dibben.

Fred was a year older than Joe Ware, and had started work a year later, at fourteen, as a fitter's mate on the old District Line. *He* loved trains, especially tube trains. He had studied the history of them closely. He knew the exact route of the old Tower Hill to Bermondsey cable-car tube, the first in the world. In fact, several of his uncles could remember travelling on it. When he had been very young he had been fascinated by their accounts of the train which actually roared and quivered underground.

Fred Dibben had started to build a model of London's Underground in the loft of an old house near the Crystal Palace where his parents rented the top floor. He had started out with a different purpose and different idea from Joe Ware—of whose existence, at the time, he had not even heard. He wanted a historical model, or models. He made his models small, but they showed clearly the development from the first tube, and even earlier—when "tubes" had really been ditches dug deep for the trains to run in, and roofed over so that they were hidden from people at street level.

Soon, Fred too had run into the problem of space.

These two lads followed their hobbies independently, until a story of Joe Ware's model of the bus transport system appeared in the *Omnibus Journal,* early in the 1920's, and was reprinted in the *Tube Times.* Fred Dibben saw it, read it to his parents with great excitement, and hurriedly wrote to the house journals to explain what he was doing.

The lad from North London and the lad from South London had met by arrangement soon afterwards—tossing up who should visit whom. Today, close friends, they would often laugh over the fact that the first time the penny had been spun, it had stuck in the crack of a pavement, and been on end.

Fred had gone to Joe. Each had gloomed over the problem of space. At the time each had been in his early twenties, and single, although each had a young lady.

They had been given a lot of publicity by this time, and a journalist in the *London Evening News,* looking for a story, had written of their difficulties, and how they would like to work together but had nowhere to go. This young reporter—who was killed in the London blitz nearly twenty years later—found himself intrigued by the pair, and became anxious to help them. He had suggested to his newspaper that they might approach the General Omnibus Company, and they had found a sympathetic General Manager. Then the reporter had had an inspiration. He suggested turning over some old buses, ready for breaking-up, to the young men, in a corner of an old bus depot.

The model makers could hardly believe their luck.

After the first flush of excitement and sensation, they had gone to work steadily and enthusiastically, finding their young ladies, soon to be their wives, ardent helpers. Gradually, the models had developed. The Underground was always on the lower deck of a bus, with the seats stripped out; the Bus Service on the top deck. They had laboured at this so long that a few officials came to see it. So did the *London Evening News* man, who was seized with another idea.

Why not open these models to the general public as well as to London transport workers, and charge a small admission fee? The model makers could give half to charity—one of the company charities—and have the rest to buy what they required to improve and extend the models. Before long, this idea was developed. Soon the Union took an interest. The museum made no profit for the two founders, for they gave every penny they could to social and benevolent funds.

Several retired bus and tube men, still interested in their life's work, gladly gave spare-time help. The schemes had developed until today it was the nearest thing to a perfect model of the whole system of surface and underground transport. Elevators, escalators, tubes, booking offices, bus and train depots, workshops, stores, vehicles—everything was to scale, and now they were planning to present an absolute replica of the whole service. The original models, on the buses, were still in existence, in a corner of the grounds of the old depot. A big airplane hanger had been re-erected nearby, and the main scale models were inside. The outside was newly painted, and read simply:

BUS & TUBE MUSEUM
J. Ware—F. Dibben
Curators

All of these years, they had continued with their jobs, moving from one stage to another, until today Old Joe Ware was a Chief Inspector of Buses, going round from route to route and depot to depot, jumping buses unexpectedly, checking the fares, making sure that no conductor could fiddle on the side. Joe was known and venerated for his human understanding, for the kindliness of his attitude. Many a young conductor caught out in "a mistake" was later called aside by Joe Ware, told the consequences of further mistakes, and given clearly to understand that a second one, if he discovered it, would lead to a report to the management, dismissal and possibly a charge.

Joe was still a tall, well-built man, but his once jet black hair was snowy white. He was clean shaven, and walked with shoulders squared; a wag once said that he looked like a retired sergeant major who had gone all benevolent.

Fred Debbin was a much shorter man, very round-shouldered—in fact the medical men of the old District Line had nearly turned him down, as deformed. He had squeezed through, become a driver in fifteen years, driven trains all over London after the merging of all the lines in the LPTB and then been offered an inspector's job, visiting the various train depots and seeing that all the amenities, such as canteens, cloakrooms, games rooms, lavatories, washrooms, clubrooms and the like were in good order. He covered both train and bus depots. He had not quite the same benevolent outlook as Joe Ware, for he had not known the same early training, but whenever he could let off a man with a caution, he would do so. But he did it roughly. He was a hard-sounding man. To look at, he was still hunch-backed, his hair was thin but nearly black, he had bright little eyes, rather shaggy eyebrows which were almost white. His face was lined and deeply etched; it was easy to believe that he had spent much of his life at the front of a train, peering along the unending dark tunnels.

Occasionally, the working schedules enabled the pair to meet for a snack or a cup of coffee. It did that day.

"If you ask me, we ought to report Higson for that kind of talk. He could make a lot of trouble." Dibbens was so sensitive to the welfare of the Board that he looked as if he hated the man who had talked to the stranger.

"I'll have a word with Higson," Ware said soothingly. "Don't make a fuss, Fred."

"One of these days someone's going to make a fuss," Fred Dibben said darkly.

In fact, he told Boman about Higson and about other big mouths. Whenever there were extremely bad cases of agitation, too, Joe Ware would tell one of the Transport policemen.

Joe and Fred were among the best eyes and ears for Superintendent Boman.

6

The Kill

AT four o'clock, Gideon's door opened, and Parsons ushered Boman in.

Boman had worked at the Yard for fifteen years, and Gideon had known him well in those old days, although they had never been close friends. Boman, a big man, had a face that was completely unexpected, especially in a policeman—it was the kind of face which made one look twice, pale and round, with startled looking china-blue eyes; almost as if a doll's face had been stuck on to the head and shoulders of a powerful man. His hair, fuzzy and thin, was now more grey than fair. His eyebrows and eyelashes were fairly well defined, but did not wholly prevent the look of the albino.

"Hallo, Beau," Gideon said, rounding his desk and shaking hands. "Good to see you again." He waved to a chair, and glanced at Parsons, who shook his head slightly; there was nothing new to report.

"Wotcher, George," Boman said. Gideon remembered his habit, from the old days, of affecting a Cockney accent. Boman sat down and Gideon pushed cigarettes across his desk. Parsons hitched up an upright chair, and sat on it back to front; it looked as if he were leaning against a pulpit. "You look as if you've been spending the summer where they get some sun. How's Kate?"

"Fine. Maggie?"

"She still tells me once a month that I was a fool to leave the Yard, and every time she sees your ugly mug in the newspapers she says if I'd had any sense, I'd be there instead of you. Shows what mistakes wives can make, doesn't it? George, I've got a problem."

"Think we can help?"

"If you can't, God knows who can." Boman lit a cigarette, and made the end of it flame. "It's not only the bus murder, that's bad enough. We've got the usual stuff to worry about on the buses and on the trains, and one nasty one that could get very unpleasant indeed." When Gideon didn't comment, Boman went on: "Very nasty one, as a matter of fact."

Gideon remembered Rogerson saying that he could not really understand what Tulson was getting at; Boman seemed to be deliberately vague, too, but it was better to let him have his head.

"Supposing we tackle the Dean murder, first," suggested Parsons.

"Suits me," agreed Boman. He sat up in his chair. "We've had a lot of these attacks on passengers—rather more than usual lately. There hasn't been any serious injury done before, but one thing's gradually taken shape, George. The same chaps have been involved in some of them. Not all—just some of them."

"Anyone answering the description of this freckled chap?" Gideon inquired hopefully.

"Yes," said Boman.

"Big help, eh, George?" Parsons put in. By now, Gideon realized that Parsons was trying to set Boman at his ease, which suggested that Boman had something on his conscience as well as on his mind.

"Could be," agreed Gideon. He glanced down at Lemaitre's report, now on his desk. Over the past twelve months there had been twenty-four attacks on passengers in buses and seventeen on passengers in trains, all of them robbery with violence, all of them either early in the morning or late at night. Few of the hauls had been big; one man had carried two hundred pounds in his pocket, after being paid off from a ship, but that was the highest. The attacks had seldom been vicious or dangerous—just enough to frighten the victim to silence, and then to knock him out.

"Out of forty-odd cases in the past year," said Boman, "seven of the victims have been able to describe the attackers. In five or six more cases we've picked up descriptions from other passengers, or from bus or tube station staff. Say twelve descriptions. Six of them mention a man with fair gingery hair and freckles. Usually he's worked with another, black-haired chap, but we can't get such a clear description of him."

Parsons put in: "It looks as if this ginger-haired chap hit too hard this time, George."

It wasn't like Parsons to stick his neck out.

"No doubt at all, in my opinion," Boman declared emphatically. "And I feel bad enough about it, George. Ought to have come to you chaps before, but I knew you were understaffed, and I thought we could tackle it."

"Couldn't have chosen a better time than this," Gideon said.

"That's something, anyhow. The way I feel, George, if we had come to you, or if we'd stepped the pressure up a bit more, we might have caught Freckles before he did this job. I've got the Deans on my conscience, that's the truth of it."

"Don't be a bloody fool."

Unexpectedly, Boman gave a quick, bright smile.

"Never did mince words, did you? Well, that's the size of the Dean job. Vic here and I have been through it with a fine-toothed comb. He wondered if this conductress could have tipped off the killers, but I don't think there's any chance of that. The same conductor has been involved three times, but that's a question of chance. I've had him watched, and he's just unlucky. None of them has shown any signs of picking up money on the side, and they would have done if they'd been tipping off the crooks. This Winifred Wylie does all right. She gets a child allowance from her husband—she's separated from him—and a good wage. I've checked her closely—eh, Vic?"

"Close as we can," Parsons said. "She's in the clear."

"Tell you what else is worrying me, George," said Boman, leaning forward earnestly and stubbing out his cigarette. "If I'd co-operated with you chaps we could have had a lot more publicity, and the fact that several people have seen this Freckles would have been in the papers. If I'd even thought they'd turn out to be killers—"

He broke off.

Gideon felt a sense of shock which put him off his balance. Boman was absolutely right. There was indeed danger to this conductress—and he, Gideon, had not given it a thought. It was always bad to overlook an obvious possibility; this one was worse than usual, because it had been staring him in the face.

"The danger is, they might try to stop her from talking," Boman went on at last.

Gideon, recovering, said cautiously: "It's certainly possible. Where is she?"

"On duty. She starts at two and works right through to the last 176—she's doing an hour's overtime every day this week. I'm having her watched, mind you. I've got one of our chaps riding with her all the way. Shouldn't think there would be any trouble, but you might have your uniformed chaps keep an eye on that particular bus."

"I will," promised Gideon. "Half a mo'." He looked across at Lemaitre, who was busy writing. "Get that, Lem?"

"Yep."

"Fix it, will you?"

"Yep." Lemaitre stretched out for a telephone.

"Thanks," said Boman. Now he shifted back in his chair more comfortably. "The next thing's only just a possibility, George—wouldn't like to put it higher."

"Go on."

"We've had well over a hundred deaths in front of tube trains in the past four years," said Boman. "In a few cases the inquest verdict has been suicide. In the others it's been accident. I'm not sure it wouldn't be a good thing to check back on those cases, and find out if any of them could be connected. Easy way to commit murder, if you're set on it and if you choose the right moment. I've got all the case records here. You've had copies, but—"

"No reason why we shouldn't have accepted the verdicts," Gideon said. And there was no reason why the Yard hadn't pondered over them, as Boman had, either.

"Mind you, there isn't any reason to think they *are* connected. It's just that I'm trying to make sure we don't miss anything." Boman emphasized that with a wag of his forefinger. "Everything else is under control, I think—we get the usual crop of windows broken, seats slashed, advertisements torn out, funny thing how vandals *have* to do something, isn't it? Had three or four cases of girls being molested on buses, and in carriages. Didn't get everyone, but two chaps are inside for assault. Bit of bag snatching and pocket picking but . . ." Boman went on for what seemed a long time, until suddenly he squared his shoulders and the tone of his voice changed. "There is one other thing, George."

"Yes?"

"You know as well as I do that we London Transport cops have a bigger variety of work to do than you chaps," went on Boman. "One of the jobs I was asked to organize a few months ago was political. I mean, keeping a watch on political activities at the bus stations and the train depots. Keeping our ears to the ground, that is. I've got one or two old trusties helping me—you ever been to the Bus and Tube Model Museum out at Greenwich?"

"I took the kids there once," Gideon said.

"It's run by a couple of old timers who get about the whole London area, visiting all the depots and stations. They've told me that this strike talk is hotting up. And we know that every depot and bus garage has a nucleus of trouble-makers. Every one," Boman emphasized.

"Strike committees, you mean?"

"Yes and no," answered Bowman. "Trouble-*makers*—always spreading rumours, complaining about overtime, keeping the bus and train crews and servicemen on edge."

"You've got about sixty thousand on the staff, haven't you?"

"Nearly eighty thousand."

"Bound to have some trouble-makers, whether communist or not, among that lot."

"Yes, but it seems to have got worse lately. Much worse. Much more talk. There hasn't been any serious labour trouble for a year or more, and my chaps report a kind of effervescence, if you see what I mean. They're afraid something will break, pretty soon. The union's all right. It's wild-cat strikes which might worry us."

Gideon did not speak.

"I put my report through to Colonel Tulson, last week," went on Boman, and suddenly Tulson's ambiguity with Rogerson became understandable. "He's talked to Corrington about it—Corrington's practically the boss of London Transport since the chairman's been so ill. And Tulson came back to me about it this morning. Said that as we were going to have to work together over the Dean inquiry, why not work together on this?"

There was a touch of irony in this situation which amused Gideon, and put him in a happier frame of mind, but he showed no outward sign. Instead, he left Boman's words hang in the air for a few seconds, and when he spoke it was an expressionless voice:

"We can't do anything about strikes and labour troubles, Beau. You know that."

"Oh, I know that. I told Tulson so." Boman was anxious to put himself in the right. "But you can do a lot that we can't—make inquiries about some of the trouble-makers, check transcripts of what they say, make sure that they don't step over the line."

"I'll have a word with the Special Branch on this one," promised Gideon. "We can't really step in unless anyone actually breaks the law, and these groups in factories and depots all over the country usually know just how far they can go. Tell Tulson I'll be back to you on this subject in a few days will you?"

"I certainly will," Boman said. He looked much happier, now that this was off his chest, and clapped his hands together rather in Lemaitre's manner.

"Having much pilfering or petty thieving?" Gideon inquired.

"Nothing we can't handle," Boman said quickly. "There's always a bit—bound to be, among eighty thousand workers and over a hundred depots!"

Gideon smiled dutifully.

"Just one other thing while I'm here, George," Boman said. "The Oval Test Match. It's going to be a big crowd, the Aussies have attracted a lot of attention and there is a good chance that this will decide the rubber. We'd better start liaison on that right away."

"You, us and Uniform," Gideon said. "We'll get into it. That the lot?"

"Isn't that enough?"

"To be going on with," Gideon agreed.

After Boman had gone, Parsons stood up and leaned against the mantelpiece. Gideon made one or two notes. Lemaitre had gone out of the office, to talk to *Information* about the special watch to be kept on Winifred Wylie's bus. Parsons waited, with that good humoured patience which was characteristic of him. When at last Gideon looked up, Parsons said:

"You ought to be a public relations officer, George."

"No more soft soap," said Gideon. "Boman was more worried than there seemed any cause to be."

"Knew he ought to have worked together with us a long time

ago," remarked Parsons. "Funny thing, how these groups and the Country forces and even the Divisions seem to think it's *infra dig* to call on us early in a job. There's one thing I'd like but I didn't suggest it then—hoped Boman would come up with it, first."

"What is it?"

"Ought to have a composite picture of this Freckles chap—get one made up by the Identikit chaps—I've got the description here." Parsons tapped his pocket. "The trouble is, Sanderson's on holiday, and we haven't got another top man in the department. Can we get someone from outside?"

"Yes," said Gideon. "Try one of the newspapers. The Wylie woman should be able to help a lot. Lay it on for tomorrow, will you? And arrange for Mrs. Wylie to be free whenever we want her."

"Right," said Parsons. "The quicker I can lay my hands on this so-and-so—"

He didn't finish.

"The conductress *is* being looked after now, anyhow," said Gideon, and felt gloomy again for a moment. "I'd missed it."

"Could see you had," said Parsons, and gave his almost smug smile. "I'd seen the possibility, George—I've had one of our chaps on her bus since it left the depot. See how well you train your subordinates!"

Gideon found himself laughing.

Winifred Wylie did not find very much to laugh about that day. On the previous night, her sleep had been often interrupted by the mind picture of that bleeding head; and the picture kept coming to her now. She was blaming herself. If she hadn't taken the fares from the two men on the platform. If she had only gone up to the top deck to make sure that everything was all right.

She thought about the two orphans, and her own child.

Being a coloured worker in London wasn't all honey. Most of

the native London men and woman were all right, but a few were positively hostile, and others snubbed you at every opportunity. Some of the Jamaican men had a very rough time in London. Today, however, everyone—Jamaican or white—had gone out of their way to have a word with her. Two men and a woman who had never been known to say a word to a coloured worker, had actually spoken to her warmly, telling her not to worry—guessing at her feelings, sharing them. That was the big relief, and she had the instinctive sense to realize that in the long run it would prove more important than the short-term anxieties. But anxious she was.

She was especially watchful of men passengers, but not because she thought there was the slightest possibility of the two men boarding the bus again. Her sense of perception and insight had been heightened. Nearing some traffic lights, she saw two men running for the bus, and for a moment one of them looked like the ginger-haired man. Her heart thumped. But as one after the other they jumped on to the platform she saw that this "ginger" man was nearer forty than twenty, and there wasn't really any similarity except in build.

Every now and again a big man got on, and at the next stop a man on his own got off.

There were more big men on their own for longer distances than usual. It wasn't often a passenger stayed: they stopped on right across the West End, from Tottenham Court Road to Trafalgar Square, the Strand and Waterloo Bridge. Were the police watching her?

Rush hour drove all these thoughts out of her mind in a frenzy of activity. Every rush hour seemed the same. After a quiet, easy spell, men and women descended on the buses like an avalanche. Streets comfortably filled with people suddenly became a seething mass. Little groups at the bus stops swelled to enormous queues, heads turning, eyes strained for each bus. This was her great testing time, and every day the fear that she would not be able to cope engulfed her, but she fought it back.

Frail old women, gentle old men, impatient middle-aged

people, too many people carrying parcels, young boys, young girls. "Threepenny, please." "Fourpenny." "Tanner, please." "All the way." "Mind my foot, clumsy." "Can you change a *pound?*" Ting, ting, ting, swaying, pushing, upstairs, downstairs, hands hot with coins, leather bag heavy against her hip. "Move along, please." "But there's room on top, I saw a seat."

Then gradually, the pressure eased, and peace returned.

The last trip across London from Catford was fairly quiet, except for short-distance picture-palace passengers. Nearing Kilburn, on that last trip, she saw two men standing in the darkness at the bus stop where she had picked up the two youths. Her heart began to beat very fast, but when the bus stopped she saw that they were older men. They got on without saying anything to her. One was funny to look at, with a big, round, pale face, and eyes rather like those of a white china doll.

At last the bus turned into the garage. Legs and back aching, Winifred went across to the cashier to turn in her takings, the ticket machine and other equipment. While she was doing this, she noticed the man speaking to the Night Superintendent. When her money had been checked and the form filled in, she turned to go and found the Night Superintendent, Mr. Charlesworth, standing with the passenger.

"Just a minute, Mrs. Wylie," Charlesworth said. He was a small, pale man who always looked tired. "This is Superintendent Boman of the Commission Police."

Her heart dropped, because she so wanted to rest.

"Glad to know you, Mrs. Wylie." Boman shook hands. "I just want you to know that we're watching you as a matter of routine—don't want you to be worried if you see some of our men about."

It was a relief.

"Just possible these chaps we want live near here and you might spot them," Boman went on with easy assurance. "If you do, we'll have someone close at hand. Tomorrow—" He told her what was now proposed about the composite portrait, thanks largely to her own description, and she was glad to promise to look at the Identikit picture when it was finished. "Still sure you will recognize this man?" inquired Boman.

"Yes, sir, I am quite sure I can."

"That's the main thing," said Boman.

When she left the garage a man who had been a passenger on the last bus followed her. She had an uneasy feeling because of this. Why should the police think it necessary to travel on her bus, and follow her wherever she went? It was almost as if they suspected *her* of committing some crime. Was that possible? She hated the thought, and yet faced it—and she also accepted the possibility that the police thought she was in some kind of danger.

Though why should anyone want to hurt—?

She broke off at that stage in her thinking, because at heart she knew quite well why the killer might want to hurt her. It was the awareness of danger which had lurked in the depths of her consciousness all day, the talk with the policeman with the moon-like face had only confirmed it. She *was* in danger—and the police knew it.

At least, they were watching her; there was really nothing to fear.

She went into the terrace house on the outskirts of Willesden, where she rented a room. It was a tiny one, and she had to share the bathroom and lavatory with several other Jamaican people who lived here, but the room itself was clean, there was space for a little armchair as well as her single bed, and the baby's cot. When she was on late turns, the child spent the night with Mrs. Pinello on the floor below. She rang Mrs. Pinello's bell, and went in to peep at her son, who was sleeping in his usual position—head well back, and lips parted. She was a little worred about the way Jo always seemed to breathe through his mouth at night; it was something she must see a doctor about.

"Will you stay with us and have a cup of tea, Winnie?" Mrs. Pinello asked.

"I'll go and undress and treat myself to a cup of tea in bed," Winifred Wylie said. "Good night, and thank you."

"It's certainly a pleasure to look after your boy. Such a well-behaved baby, Winnie. Don't you worry at all about him."

People were so good.

Winnie unlocked the door of her own room, put her fingers automatically on the switch, and stepped inside, narrowing her eyes against the brightness of the single ceiling light. She half turned, to close and lock the door, as she always did. She heard nothing and saw no sign of danger—until, from behind her, hands clutched at her throat.

She began to scream; but choking pressure cut the sound short.

7

Failure

GIDEON was alone in the office, at half past eleven next morning, feeling reasonably well satisfied with himself and with the way things were going. He had done the morning briefing. Only two major crimes had been committed during the night, and his men were still not stretched too tightly. He had spent half an hour with Hobbs—it was easy to think of him as "young Hobbs"—about the murder of the Soho prostitute. They were after a sex killer, undoubtedly, and there were some indications that it might be a man who lived on the girl's earnings. Hobbs had been admirably objective about the whole thing, and if he realized that Lemaitre had given him the case deliberately, so as to make sure that he tackled one of the beastliest jobs on the seamy side of London life, he showed no sign of it. He was back in the pathological laboratory, checking over the ugly wounds.

Ringall had come in briefly, bumbling but delighted with the fingerprints on the envelope, the bus tickets and the locket, even more delighted that a fragment of a print on the bus ticket found in Bournemouth coincided with one found in Brighton. The conductors had been identified, and their prints set aside. The remaining one must be the passenger's. There was good reason to hope that the police had the prints of the Seaside Strangler. The car park attendants in Brighton and Bournemouth were to be questioned about anyone who had parked a car and then put something from their pockets into a waste bin, but the chances of results from that were small. It might be months before the police could find the man whom those prints fitted, might not be until after he had killed and killed again, for there was nothing in Records about them. But at least it was a fillip, and had filled Ringall with new hope.

Lemaitre had checked the files which Parsons and Boman had left with Gideon, and Gideon was most interested in the deaths which occurred from falling in front of tube trains. If there really were any grounds for suspecting a series of murders, this was very ugly indeed. He kept telling himself that there were no grounds, and that Boman had been making his conscience work overtime, but nevertheless it was a possibility. The more he studied the deaths, the more he thought that three of them could be connected.

It might be a tenuous association of ideas, but there were two youngish women and a middle-aged man who had died in three different Central London stations. Each death fall had been from a spot near an exit. In each case the verdict at the inquest had been suicide; the most recent was three and a half years ago.

Gideon let this soak into his mind, and put the files away. He needed to find out more about these "suicides."

Parsons had been in, to say that he had brought an artist from the *Daily Globe* to work on the Identikit picture from the various descriptions. The *Globe* had cheerfully agreed—provided it could claim the kudos of having its man work for the police—that the picture could be distributed to all the newspapers and the news agencies. The Wylie woman's opinion would be the most important.

"Might go along and see how the chap is getting on," Gideon mused to himself, and one of his telephone bells rang. He lifted it at once.

"Gideon." He was asked to hold on for someone from GH Division—the Division which covered the Willesden area—but he did not think very seriously about it. Instead, he doodled the word "strike" on a sheet of blotting paper. The part of the police in strikes or in any kind of political demonstration was always tricky, and he could see a lot of dangers in this one. He had a feeling that someone—possibly Tulson—was deliberately trying to involve the Yard so as to avoid taking part in political issues. At that point in his thinking, he reminded himself that he was taking exactly the same attitude to the Transport Commission police as T.C. did towards the Yard.

Was no one free from this kind of self-interest?

"Hallo, George." It was Ingleby, the Superintendent at GH. "I've an ugly job here, one you won't like at all."

Gideon said: "Try me." But on the instant he felt a weight of depression.

"That coloured bus conductress—Winifred Wylie."

"Yes."

"Strangled."

Gideon muttered: "Oh God." His lips were dry. "But I thought—" It was a bigger shock than he had had for a long time, and he hadn't really reacted yet. He felt stunned. "She was being watched."

"She was. My chaps."

Gideon said: "Strangled?"

"The killer was waiting for her in her flatlet. Got in with a skeleton key." When Gideon didn't interrupt, Ingleby went on: "The landlady let her sleep in this morning, as she thought, but went up to see her when she wasn't about by eleven o'clock. The landlady looks after the child—"

Another child.

"Mrs. Wylie usually goes down to the landlady about eight o'clock. She takes the baby up to her own room, stays until one o'clock, then has her dinner and goes to the depot." Ingleby paused. "She was on the bed."

"Just strangled?"

"Yes."

"Who knows about this?"

"I've a police surgeon and three men on the way, but I haven't told *Information.* I don't want the newspapers to get hold of it too soon."

"No," Gideon said. He felt as if he were being choked. "I'll send Parsons. Does Boman know?"

"No. He saw her last night—before my chaps followed her."

"Was her house watched?"

Ingleby answered: "We had a man there an hour before she was due home, and no one was seen to go in. It was after dark when she got home. I've been talking to the man on duty at the house, and he says he saw no one come out. Scratches on the room door suggest a skeleton key was used—just a piece of wire would do—and the killer could have escaped over the roofs and climbed down further along the street."

"Oh," said Gideon.

"My chap might have fallen down on the job," Ingleby said. "There's no way of being sure, but I'll watch him."

Gideon grunted.

He himself hadn't given enough thought to this—both Boman and Parsons had got there before him—and a man could easily have slipped up through not taking the danger seriously. He himself had not really believed that the danger was very great, murder to keep the victim silent was still a rare thing in England.

It wasn't any use blowing his top at Ingleby.

"All right," he said. "I'll tell Parsons. Do you want any help?"

"I think I'd like someone from *Fingerprints,* and from *Photography*. I can manage the rest."

"I'll fix it," promised Gideon. He rang off, moistened his lips and hesitated, staring across at Lemaitre's empty desk. Why the hell wasn't Lemaitre there when he was wanted? Gideon lifted a telephone and Lemaitre came bustling in, grinning as he so often was.

"George, have you heard this one? Two men and a blond were having a night out when—*what the hell?*"

"Get Boman on the line," Gideon said, and spoke into his own telephone. "Tell Mr. Parsons to come in right away. He banged down the receiver, and watched as Lemaitre talked into the telephone, eyeing him closely all the time. Lemaitre covered the telephone.

"What is it?"

"That conductress was strangled."

"*Gawd.*"

Parsons said: "Want me, George?" from round the door.

"Come in, right away," said Gideon. He lifted the receiver again, and rapped the platform up and down. The operator answered swiftly. "*Fingerprints,* and have *Photography* on the line waiting for me." He held on, as Lemaitre said: "Boman's on this line." Gideon picked up another telephone with his left hand, and talked as he stared at Parsons. "Beau, you were right. Winifred Wylie was strangled during the night."

Parsons caught his breath.

"She was—" Boman began, and then his voice rose. "But I only saw her—"

"Ingleby wants us to send someone from *Prints* and *Photography*, and they're going over with Vic Parsons now. You want to go?"

"I—I suppose I'd better. Yes, of course."

"If the Press gets a sniff of it, we'd better be careful what we say," said Gideon. "Will you join Parsons at the flatlet?"

"Yes."

"Right." Gideon rang off, seeing Parsons at one of Lemaitre's telephones. Parsons was ordering his murder bag to be taken down to his car, and rang off almost at once. "Tell Ingleby that we'll need house-to-house questioning, and we may be after this freckled man," Gideon said. "That Identikit chap finished yet?"

"He's made a few stabs, but none of the victims have seen

the result yet."

"Fix it soon." Then Gideon changed his mind. "No, have the drawings sent in here. Lem can get some of the victims to come here and look at them."

"Right away," said Parsons, and went out.

Several people indirectly connected with the Yard's urgent problem were at the *Bus & Tube Model Museum* that afternoon. It was very busy. Two parties of school children were there, including Jack and Jill Kenworthy, rather too young for the occasion, and a younger brother of Arty Gill, aged fourteen, very different from his senior, and always fascinated by trains. He caught Fred Dibben's eye.

Fred's real love was the train side of the museum, of course, and he could spot a train enthusiast very early in a tour. It was the one afternoon of the week when he and Joe Ware were at the Museum together, each taking the same rest day so as to coincide. Joe was taking a party of adults round, most of them student conductors and drivers on the bus routes.

A man of about thirty, dressed in a pale-brown suit which needed pressing, with receding fair hair which formed a very pronounced widow's peak, attached himself to Fred Dibben's party, looking rather out of place because most of the others were school children. He had a slight scar on his right nostril, and from time to time fingered the scar. He asked no questions—the children fired them like machine-gun bullets—but drank in the answers. He showed special attention when Dibben described the actual lay-out and position of some of the stations, and explained that many of them were practically identical, as far as exits and entrances, staircases, escalators and elevators were concerned.

"Please, sir," a boy asked, "which is the deepest part of the Underground?"

"Hampstead Station, son." Dibben's blunted forefinger pointed. "Goes down over 180 feet there, it does—there's the deepest lift shaft in the system, there."

"In all London?"

"That's what they tell me," said Dibben, and hurried on: "Goes as deep there as Nelson's column goes up. Can anyone tell me how tall Nelson's Column is?"

"Hundred and eighty feet, of course," said a lad with thoughtful grey eyes.

"Please sir—how *fast* do the trains go?"

"Fast enough to make a mess of you if you get in front of one, my lad. Twenty miles an hour in the tubes—"

"Only *twenty?*"

"It sounds like a hundred to me," a boy confided.

"Well, it's twenty on average—can go a bit more, of course. Out in the open they go at forty miles an hour, mind you."

"Please sir—"

"Never stop asking questions, do they?" Dibben remarked to the man in brown. The man half smiled, and fingered the little scar on his nostril.

"How many people travel on the railway every day, sir?"

"Well, I've never actually *counted* them," began Dibben, and after a pause, won a burst of laughter. He joined in heartily. "Getting on for two million a day, and every one has to have a ticket. Just think how much waste paper that means! Now supposing you stop asking me questions and let me tell *you* something."

He stood with the children on a platform above a huge relief model of the Underground system, which showed where it went deep and where it became shallow, where it emerged from the tunnels, where the depots were—all out of the tunnel areas, of course—where the carriages and engines "went to sleep". Although he had told this story thousands of times, he did not intone it, but talked in an interested manner, dropping in odd pieces of information. He stood in front of a panel which had dozens of press buttons on it, and kept putting his finger on a button. Immediately, one of the features of the model lit up.

"There's the depot at New Cross," he said. "That holds

over five hundred carriages at night—have a big night staff servicing them—"

"Please, what does service mean?"

"Looking after them so that they're ready for work next day," Dibben elaborated. "Over four thousand cars altogether."

"Have you got four thousand cars *here?*" The man with the scar sounded startled.

"Care to count 'em?"

The children roared with laughter, except one lad who began solemnly:

"One, two, three, four—"

"Put a sock in it. There are the tunnels," Dibben pointed out. "Look." He pressed a switch, a tiny train began to move out near Ealing, gathered speed and disappeared into a tunnel. "Ninety-eight miles of tunnel altogether," went on Dibben. "Two hundred and fifty-eight miles of track altogether—bit too much for your back yard, eh?"

"How long's *that* long tunnel?" a child asked, pointing.

"I hoped you'd ask that, my boy. That's the longest train tunnel in the world, maybe it's the longest tunnel of any kind. Seventeen miles, all the way from East Finchley"—he flashed a light north of the Thames—"to Morden." A light flashed south of the river. "Now, let's have a look at these stations. Take Piccadilly—"

He did not notice the man with the scar paying very close attention to his description of Piccadilly Station, the fact that over half a million people used the station every day. Soon afterwards this man slipped a shilling into Dibben's hand, and went off, but the children continued to ply him with their questions.

Joe Ware was having just as good a time.

He stood in a similar kind of position, but with a surface map of London stretched out in front of him, the roads dotted with tiny models of red buses, a few green double-deckers, many more single deckers in green. The area extended a very long way, and there were arrows pointing to terminal points too far out of London for the model. Joe was rather more mechanical in his narrative. The area covered over two thousand square miles within a radius of twenty-five miles from Charing Cross. There were five thousand five hundred and fifty red buses and nearly a thousand green ones, and a couple of hundred single deckers. Most of the questions he was asked came from a green-eyed, eager little Irishman, who had announced gaily that his name was Paddy O'Neil, and that he had just become a conductor on the Number 15 route.

Also there was a man whom Ware knew slightly, an electrical engineer, who specialized on maintenance and travelled bus and tube districts freely. He had a ten year old son with him, and paid particularly close attention, but asked no questions.

"Which is the longest route, would you say, dad?" the Irishman asked.

"Number 133, on Sundays. Twenty-three-point-seventy-five miles, that is. That's the Central line. On weekdays the 65 from Ealing to Leatherhead does nineteen-point-seventy-five."

"And how many miles do the buses run altogether?"

"Two hundred and twenty million nine hundred thousand per annum." Joe Ware's answer drew the expected gasp of astonishment.

Paddy O'Neil seemed to drink it all in.

The electrician was particularly attentive to the talk about the various depots.

When the two parties were finished, Joe Ware and Fred Dibben left the next tour to two retired conductors, who enjoyed the spare time job, and went to have a cup of tea in a small café adjoining.

"I had a word with Superintendent Boman today," Ware said. "He came over to see me, special. They're getting worried about the Action Committees, Fred. Very worried."

"So they damn well should," Dibben said.

The Action Committees were known to exist, and some of their members were also known, but for the most part they met in secret, and instructed their members to complain, and to seize upon any grievance, no matter how small, and work it up. They formed, of course, a political body, but the instructions which had gone to every member were positive and clear:

> *"While no opportunity for creating the conditions for unrest should be missed members must at all times obey the laws of the country and the regulations of the Board. Failure to do this will be met with instant dismissal from the Committee as such action would get the Committee into disrepute."*

"Nuts to that," said Higson, the leader of the Committee at Willesden.

He had two friends, who travelled the whole area of the Transport Board on special service work—they were electricians—who agreed with him fully. They had their own ideas as to the best way to create trouble, serious trouble, which would win a lot of sympathy and would certainly start strikes at some of the depots.

Like all Action Committee members, they were quiet, unobtrusive workers, and very few people even suspected their activities. Certainly Joe Ware did not realize that one of them had been so attentive at the Museum that afternoon.

Later on that same day, Gideon and Lemaitre looked down at an Identikit version of the face of the man who *might* look like Freckles. Neither of them could know, though they suspected, that there was very little likeness at all; that it would be a long time before the expert could make this fit into the descriptions which had already been given. The one witness who might have helped with the short cut was gone.

This was going to be a hell of a case.

During the rest of that working day, another warm one, the Yard, the Divisions, the Transport Police and the newspapers all worked together on the hunt for the double murderer. Gideon had seldom known a greater sense of united purpose, and that did a little to ease the nagging sense of responsibility which he felt. It was no use telling himself that he did the very best he could. He had fallen down on this job, and that little Jamaican woman had paid for it.

It was a bigger task than usual for him to thrust thought of the case aside, and to concentrate on the others, but by the middle of the afternoon he had things more in perspective.

Outside, Londoners were getting ready to go home. It was going to be a miserable journey. Trains and buses would be hot and packed. The great octopus of London Transport would move all its tentacles to try to contain the working millions until they were disgorged from the outlying stations, but a hot day always made the situation worse. Somehow or other the better part of seventy thousand workers in the buses and twenty thousand in the tubes were geared to cope with the millions of the shifting population, and every tube station would be crowded from four o'clock on. The homegoing rush was always worse than the incoming one.

At one of these stations there *might* be a killer, waiting to push someone in front of a train.

Hildegard Delancy had no idea that he was being watched.

In spite of his elegant name, he was an ordinary London suburban office worker, unmarried, although now aged thirty-two. He lived at home with his widowed mother; the Delancys seldom got married early. He was not particularly well-dressed or good-looking, but he struggled to make sure that he kept up appearances. He wore a bowler hat with a narrow brim, carried a furled umbrella—thundery showers had been forecast—and wore a clerical grey suit.

He was in the accounts department of Chindini & Company.

The office block was in Long Acre, and the most direct way for him to get to his Hounslow home was on the Piccadilly Line, so he always walked to Leicester Square Station. Tonight, the crowds seemed thicker than ever. The men particularly looked very hot. The girls were cooler, many in the short sleeves and short skirts which his mother deplored so much—but he was not so convinced as he used to be. Some of the girls looked very nice. They *had* breasts, and could hardly conceal them, could they? Supposing some of them did use brassieres which made them a bit more obvious—did it really matter? There was one girl he noticed in particular, as he had for some weeks past. They saw each other most nights. He had followed her from her office building tonight, walking just behind her—she worked somewhere in a huge block in Long Acre, as he had noticed a few days ago.

She was a few yards ahead of him.

She had nice legs, tanned beautifully. The skirt of her blue, white and red striped dress—vertical stripes—was what his mother would call "disgracefully short." Certainly her knees showed, and an inch of her legs above them. She always sat with her legs close together, rather demurely. She wasn't really tall: rather dumpy, in fact. She wore a sleeveless dress, and her arms were as brown as her face and shoulders—he thought that she must do a lot of swimming or sun-bathing. It would be wonderful to—to see her sunbathing. The curious sense of guilt that his mother had contrived to give him covered him with a kind of confusion then, but he fought it back. He would like to see her—without any clothes on. He would like to sleep with her.

If he caught up with her, he would see the way her breasts strained against the cotton dress, as if determined not to be confined. He would like to touch her.

She had a little turned up nose, and nice lips and beautiful teeth. Now and again he had seen her smile. For some time he had been plucking up his courage to speak to her. He would have done so, except that last week she had come with a youth from the same office, and he had thought that it meant she was having an *affaire*, but the youth hadn't shown up for some days. If he could only keep pace until they were on the platform, he would have his chance. The crowd would push them together, there would be no way of stopping that. If they got into the same carriage—sometimes they did—he could make some odd remark, some little thing to make her laugh, and instead of going past South Ealing, where she got out—he would go out with her, and—well, there was no *harm* in it, was there?

Hildegard Delancy had no idea that his attitude was so far behind the times that very few people of his own age, or even younger, would believe that he was going through this curious kind of exquisite torment.

He kept close to the girl at the station. Both had season tickets, and showed them. She popped hers back into her handbag. She glanced round as she did so, shyly—*shyly?*—saw him, and smiled. Quite suddenly, they were standing together on the escalator. Hundreds of others were about them, but to Delancy no one else was there. He touched her arm. He wished she were behind him, so that he could lean back a little. They reached the foot of the moving stairs and she stumbled. He took her arm quickly. She gave him a very bright smile—she was *beautiful.*

"Thank you."

"It's a pleasure."

"I caught my heel."

"It's easy to do."

He was still holding her arm, and she didn't take it away.

"It's a good job you were there."

"I'm very glad I was."

"You always catch this train, don't you?"

"If I can."

So she had noticed.

"Where do you live?"

"Out at Hounslow East."

"That's four stops further along the line than mine."

"I know."

"Really?"

"Yes, I—I've often noticed you."

"Have you *really?*"

They were among hundreds on the platform now. People were pushing, edging, poking with their elbows, treading on toes, getting out of the way of brief-cases. The whole platform was a seething mass of homegoing Londoners, packed tight, and yet Delancy was hardly aware of it. The scene and the experience had become part of life; it was rather like breathing. For another, *he had his arm round the girl's waist,* and she was looking up and smiling.

Someone pushed him a little nearer the edge, but he did not notice. He noticed only that he had to hold her a little more tightly. He felt the soft, swelling weight just above his thumb.

"If we get nearer the front we might be lucky."

"Shall we?"

"I'll lead the way."

He held her tightly, and pulled her while he pushed towards the end of the platform and towards the edge. Someone pushed him again. He didn't really notice. His umbrella was a nuisance, he had it hooked over his left arm. He kept thinking about the pressure against his thumb, and wished desperately that they were alone. She was the loveliest little thing he had ever seen, and in spite of the heat, she looked so clean and cool. She had wonderful blue eyes and her hair, as fine as silk, was a golden colour.

They were closer to the edge. He was forging his way forward with more self-assurance than he had ever shown before, some kind of protective instinct stirring in him. She was very close. He heard a rumbling sound of an approaching train—they *had* to get in this one. If he failed he would fail her, too. He had to show her what he could do, how much in control he was. He looked along the platform and saw the lights of the train. He twisted his head round, to look at her.

"We'll make it."

She wasn't looking at him, though, she was staring at someone behind him. Unexpectedly, she said in a sharp voice:

"What do you think you're doing?"

Was she talking to *him?* Did she resent it after all? Was he being too familiar—?

He heard the roaring of the train. He felt pressure on his shoulder, and saw a man's hand on *her* shoulder, as if he were pushing her. Then he felt himself being pushed towards the edge of the platform, felt a sharp pain behind his legs, and seemed to lose all control of them. *The train roared.* He was falling, he was falling in front of those thundering wheels. He saw the face of the driver, saw the terror on the man's face. That roaring was like the terrible sound of the end of the world. Instinctively, he thrust the umbrella out in front of him, to try to push back—an idiotic move against the train. Brakes were squealing, the driver's mouth was wide open.

The train caught the end of the umbrella. It was wrenched out of Delancy's grip. The driver disappeared. The red side of the carriage slid past him, then the windows, the people inside, jostling, already pushing towards the doors. The brakes stopped squealing and the engine only whined. His wrist hurt where he had been holding the umbrella.

A door slid open in front of him, and people pushed their way out. Someone with a metallic voice said: "*Mind the gap please.*" A moment later: "*Do not crowd in the doors please there will be another train immediately after this one.*"

The girl was pushing him in the back.

"Get in," she said desperately. "Get in."

He had been standing, just standing. Now, people pushed and he was thrust forward. But for the girl's support, he would have fallen. There were three empty seats. She guided him towards one, and he dropped into it. That had been terrible,

terrible. *He had nearly fallen in front of the train.*

Suddenly, the girl was leaning forward, pushing close to him. The neckline of her dress drooped, he could see the frilly edge of a brassier, he could see . . .

"Are you all right?" she asked urgently. "Are you all right? You look awful."

8

New Friends

AFTER a long time, Delancy managed to say: "Don't worry about me. I'm all right." He looked into the girl's deep violet eyes and dimly understood the concern in them, real anxiety for him. But at that moment he could not appreciate its significance; he was still so frightened. The roaring of the train against the walls as he sat here so still, was different from the menacing sound of it hurtling into the station, but to him it was just the same: the sound of approaching death. He could picture the gargoyle-like face of the driver. He could feel the pressure against his back, and the kick against his knees. Worst of all, there was the awful feeling, of horror and of hopelessness, as he had fallen forward.

The girl had saved him.

"The girl—and his umbrella. His gamp. He felt like shrieking with laughter. Saved by a gamp!

The girl was suddenly pressed against him, as the train slowed down; then there was another rush of passengers. She straightened up, but had her hands on his shoulder, to steady herself.

"You're sure?"

"Yes."

"You're very pale."

"It was—it was a bit of a scare."

"A bit of?"

"I'm all right now."

"You look—" the girl broke off, and muttered something which sounded like: "It doesn't matter." At last Delancy became aware of the fact that the people near them were curious, obviously listening, and that the girl had realized it at the same time. She straightened up, and took one hand away from him, but the other stayed. He looked straight at her. His head was on a level with her breast. He looked at the unblemished, golden-brown skin of her rounded arm, and his gaze travelled along it to her hand; it was small; tiny; all her skin was lovely. It would be, all over her body.

He must be feeling better.

The middle-aged man sitting next to him got up. The girl dropped into the vacated seat, and smoothed the hem of her skirt nearer her knees. Delancy was sorry that her hand was no longer on his shoulder.

She leaned towards him.

"Your umbrella," she said.

"What?"

"Look at your umbrella."

He glanced at his left hand. The handle of the umbrella was clutched in it, firmly, and he had not realized that, but it was broken off just below the fastening ring, so that all he held was a splintered handle. It looked so silly.

He laughed.

"That won't keep out much rain!"

"You'd better leave it."

"Keep it as a souvenir, I think."

"Some souvenir."

He nodded. He felt suddenly, overwhelmingly tired. Strength seemed to ooze out of his arms and legs, and he closed his eyes. The roaring was still in his ears, but it was like death groaning away, defeated. He remembered being knocked off his bicycle once, when a boy. He had banged his head on the kerb, and lost consciousness. When he had recovered, he had felt something like he did now. The swaying of the train was comforting. The nearness of the girl, and the touch of her shoulder and her arm, were warm, welcome, pleasing. The train stopped again; now it was beginning to empty, there was much less crush. He opened his eyes and glanced at the girl, seeing that she was staring at him intently.

"I thought you'd fainted," she said.

"I assure you I'm all right."

She leaned closer, and her lips nearly touched his ear.

"Did you know that—" she broke off.

"What?"

"Some man *pushed* you."

"It was an awful crush."

"He pushed you deliberately."

Her breath was warm against his ear, her voice raised so that he could hear it above the clatter of the train.

"No one would—" he began.

"But he did! I saw him, he—he pushed me away when I tried to help you. He was dressed in brown. I'd know him again anywhere."

"I can't believe it."

"I tell you he *did,*" the girl insisted. "I'm absolutely positive." He heard her catch her breath. "He actually tried to push you in front of that train."

It was absurd, surely—and yet he could almost feel the pressure at his shoulders, and the sudden sharp blow on the back of his knees.

"I can't believe—"

"You've got to believe it," she insisted. Then she drew back sharply, as if in alarm, and her next words sounded a long way off. "Or don't you want to believe it?"

He didn't understand what she meant.

"Of course not. It's just that I can't—"

The train was turning a bend, and the roar came much more

loudly through the small windows, but in a moment it came out of the tunnel and into the open air, into daylight after subterranean gloom. The next stop would be Barons Court. There was less roaring, although the train seemed to rock more. Daylight changed the look of the other passengers, and took something sinister out of what had happened. It did not change the girl, not really—it just revealed more clearly the absolute flawlessness of her skin, and deep violet of her eyes.

"I'll soon be at my station," she said.

"Er—yes. Yes, I suppose you will." The habit of watching her get out at South Ealing was so strong in Delancy that for a moment he did not give it a thought; and then he became acutely aware that he did not want her to go and leave him. He wanted to talk to her for a long, long time. "Look here," he said, "I—may I get out with you?"

She hesitated, and he wondered if he had really said anything which had caused her offence.

"Do you really want to?"

"Do I!"

Her eyes lit up. "I won't have to be late tonight, though. Mum and Dad are going to the pictures, it's my night for babysitting." She edged a little closer to him, and her eagerness faded, anxiety replacing it. "What are you going to do?"

"Do?"

"About being pushed."

Had he been pushed?

"We can't talk about it here," he said. "Let's wait until we get out."

"All right," she agreed.

He stepped out into the unfamiliar street when they had climbed the stairs from the platform. As he stood hesitating, the girl took his arm, and turned right, then walked along a narrow street. She seemed to know exactly where she was going, and he wondered what she had meant by saying that she wouldn't have to be late. *How* late? His mother would start worrying unless he was home by half past six, and it was a quarter past now. The evening was lovely, the sun still shone from a clear sky, but there was a breeze, and it wasn't too hot.

They came to a patch of common, as neat and tidy as a park. Dotted about the yellowing grass of this dry summer, in full view of everyone passing, were many couples. Lying down, sitting down, cuddling, hugging, necking—his mother's word was "shameful." Here and there were families, with children running about, playing ball, screaming. A radio sounded softly.

The girl did not pause. Delancy's heart began to beat very fast. Shameful it might be, but if only he dared to find a quiet spot, if only she would sit down with him, if only she would—

"Let's go over there," she said.

She pointed, and a minute or two later they were on the fringe of a little thicket of trees and bushes. Through the rich summer foliage he could see colours of clothes, and knew that couples were using each little nook. His mouth was dry.

"Do you know, I don't even know your name," she said.

She spread her short, bell-shaped skirt, and sat down on a patch of yellowing grass. Other couples were in sight here, and a boy was lying right on top of a girl; they were motionless. This girl bent her knees, and sat like a—like a dryad. She leaned on one arm, and as Delancy sat down, gave a little laugh.

"That umbrella!"

"Yes. My—my name's a bit unusual."

"Mine's not. Emily Smith!"

He found himself smiling.

"Mine is Hildegard Delancy."

"*My*," she said. "Posh."

"It's a bit too high sounding, really."

"Oh, I don't think so," she replied. "It's a bit of a mouthful. *Hilde*gard?" She echoed the short "i".

"Yes."

"I hope they don't call you Hilda!"

The old joke had been uttered so many times that Delancy hardly gave it a second thought, just laughed it off.

"No. They usually call me Gard."

"That's different, anyway." She shifted her position, leaning back, with her arms behind her, and on the ground, supporting her. The pose thrust her bosom forward, and he could hardly take his eyes off that thrusting, challenging body. "What *are* you going to do about it?"

"About what—" he began, and then made himself look into her eyes. "What *can* I do?"

"You can't just forget it."

"Well—"

"Listen, Gard, that man pushed you deliberately. I saw him, I tell you. He followed us through the crowd. As a matter of fact I noticed him because he kept picking his nose—disgusting, some people are. He had a little scar, I saw him *ever so* clearly. I thought he was just taking advantage of the lane you were making, but when we got to the edge he gave you a shove, *and* he dug his knee into the back of yours. He tried to murder you, don't you understand?"

Delancy said slowly, painfully: "If you say so it must have happened, but it just doesn't make sense."

"It would have made sense if you'd gone down in front of that train, wouldn't it? I was terrified."

"I was pretty scared myself."

"Gard, why should anyone try to kill you?"

"I can't even imagine a reason."

"There *must* be one."

Suddenly, as if with blinding comprehension, he cried: "He must have mistaken me for someone else!"

Emily Smith was still leaning back on her hands. Very slowly, she shook her head. She was smiling, but her eyes were narrowed. In a way she reminded him of his mother when she was set on something; he had often seen that kind of calculating expression.

"He had a long look at you, and he was pretty close," she said. "He meant to push Hildegard Delancy in front of that train, not anyone else. You'll have to go to the police."

Delancy didn't answer.

"Or—is there a special reason why you shouldn't?" Emily Smith demanded.

"Well, no. I don't think I'd like the fuss, and my mother certainly wouldn't, but—"

"Gard," she said, leaning forward and taking his hands in hers, "You're not mixed up in anything, are you? You read such queer things in the papers. You're not—you're *not* mixed up in any funny business, are you?"

He was so startled that at first he could only stare; and then he gave a little burst of laughter.

"Good lord, no! I'm an accountant at Chindini's—you know, the big pharmaceutical firm—drugs and things. Just an ordinary nine to five-thirty accountant. You can't really think—"

Emily was pouting a little; prettily.

"I didn't really think anything, I just wondered. You do read such a lot of funny things in the papers. And this man did come and try to push you in front of the train, you know."

"Yes, I know. I—"

Delancy broke off, realizing quite suddenly how much he owed to her. Until this moment, he had known what had happened, and understood that she had pulled him back from the train, but he had not realized exactly what it meant: that she had saved his life. But for her, he would be a mangled mess of flesh and bone on that line—they wouldn't have got him up yet. He had another flash of memory—of the incredible choking, half suffocating mob of people who had gathered on that platform a few years ago, when a woman from the office had thrown herself in front of a train. The delay had been nearly an hour, and the crowd had not been able to get on or off.

"What's the matter?" she demanded sharply.

"I've—I've just realized that I owe you my life," said Delancy, very humbly. "I want you to know that I'll never forget it. I mean that."

She was still leaning close, her lips still pouting slightly;

invitingly. He shifted his position. His arms went round her. He pressed his lips against hers, fiercely, hotly. He felt the ravishing pressure of her body against his. A flush seemed to spread throughout his body, and her body was yielding. They were in an awkward position and there was no hope of lying down with her, without a lot of shifting about, and he did not want to move. He just wanted to feel that pressure against his chest, and her lips against his, the breath from her nostrils purring against him. He hardly knew how long he stayed like that, just felt an all-consuming need of her. He quivered; not violently, not as with cold, but all over his body.

Then the physical climax came, and tension seemed to melt away. The grip of his arms relaxed. The pressure of his lips softened. He eased her away from him, but she showed no sign of wanting to free herself. He was breathing very hard; gaspingly; she was breathing softly.

Gradually, he drew further back, and opened his eyes.

"You'll never know how—how much I've wanted to do that."

She didn't respond.

"I have—really. For—weeks."

She had a faraway look in her eyes.

"Weeks?"

"Yes."

She began to smile faintly, and looked at him steadily.

"Don't be silly."

"I mean it."

"You didn't even know I existed!"

"I've watched you for ages."

She was startled. "Really?"

"Yes—honestly. You work in Long Acre, don't you? That big new building—what do they call it?"

"Assan House," she said mechanically. "You really mean you've been watching me like that?"

"I couldn't keep my eyes off you."

"Well, I'm amazed. I didn't think you really noticed me.

I—" Emily gave her little infectious laugh. Her wide lips parted easily in laughter, she had nice teeth, and was inclined to show the tip of her tongue. "I'd noticed you, too."

"Really?"

"Yes. I—"

Delancy said: "*Must* you go and baby-sit tonight?"

"'Fraid so," she replied at once. "I can't let Mum and Dad down on their one night out a week, can I? But—look, why don't you come home with me? They won't mind." She spoke with blithe assurance, but it did not occur to him that there must have been others who had gone home with her on baby-sitting night for her to be so sure that they wouldn't mind. Then she said with almost devastating frankness: "They know they can trust me! Would you like to come and take pot luck for supper?"

"Well, if you're sure—"

"Of course I'm sure! Then we can talk about what you're going to do. As a matter of fact I've got an idea that might solve the problem. One of my friends' fathers is a policeman. I've known him all my life, he's ever such a decent sort. He'll come over like a shot, if I ask him."

"I suppose it's a good idea," said Delancy. "If the man really did push me—"

"If you're saying I'm a liar, *Hilde*gard Delancy—"

"No! No, I'm sorry, I take that back." He was again afraid that he had caused offense, but saw that she was laughing.

She got up, quickly, gracefully. They stood face to face for a moment or two, and then he slid his arm round her waist and drew her close and kissed her, but there was not the same surge of passion, although there were eagerness and pleasure. This time she was breathing rather hard when he let her go.

"Do you make all your girl friends puff like that?" she demanded.

"You may not believe it," said Hildegard Delancy, "but I've never really had a girl friend. Oh, I've taken girls out now and again, but I've been swotting so hard for my exams, and—well, we're a very united family. I live at home with my mother, you see. And I've been too busy and—well, not really interested."

She was hugging his arm against her.

"Well, all I can say is you're a natural when it comes to kissing. I've never had a steady, not a real steady—not since I was sixteen, anyhow."

"How old are you now?"

"Eighteen."

"I'm afraid I'll seem very old to you."

"How old *are* you, grandpa?"

He laughed.

"Thirty-one."

"Well, I must say you don't look it," said Emily.

They did not speak again until they were in a street of fairly modern houses, each with a front garden, many gardeners busy. A woman pushing a pram said: "Hallo, Emmy," and two small boys waved to her. Delancy clutched her arm with his right hand, and the crook of the umbrella in his left, feeling conspicuous in his dark suit and bowler hat, and wondering what kind of reception they would really get.

And he wondered what his mother would say when he got home. He had always warned her if he was going to be late; if she didn't know where he was she would worry.

Oh, well, it couldn't be helped for once.

Exactly two days later, on the Saturday of that week, Gideon saw a pencilled note on his desk, marked: "From LI Division." That was one of the outer London Divisions, covering Ealing, Hanwell and a large area north of the Thames. The Superintendent in charge was Tim Corbett, one of the old timers, who would end his active police days in LI. These days he had little trouble in his largely residential and suburban manor, but he had spent some hectic years in the East End.

It being Saturday, there was less briefing than usual. Hobbs was waiting to see Gideon about the Soho sex murders, but

Ringall was down in Bournemouth, where he had gone to interview a couple who thought they had seen the dead girl and a man on the night of the murder, and remembered what the man looked like. As he hadn't called from the seaside, Ringall presumably hadn't yet had much luck. Riddell was due in about the robbery with violence job.

There was nothing new about the murder of Winifred Wylie. No one had been seen entering or leaving the house where she had lived, and there was one aspect of this which troubled Gideon, but he hadn't yet talked about it with anyone. He had a more comprehensive picture of the position on the London Transport crime situation than he had known for a long time. One thing was a considerable relief: the Transport Police Force was tightly organized, and had pilfering, wilful damage and the other commonplace crimes well under control.

But Boman was still worried by the Dean murder. And the conductress's. But for her, Dean's death would have faded out of the newspapers, now one of the Sunday sheets would be sure to take it up in a big way.

He slit open the note from Corbett, and found a pencilled note—the LI Superintendent was making sure that this was not yet a formal issue.

George,

Re your memo. about deaths from falling in front of t. trains. One of our uniformed chaps heard a queer story the other day. Man says he was pushed at Piccadilly and nearly done for. Like me to check myself? Or w'd you like one of y'r specialists on the job?

The scrawled signature was *Tim C.*

The door opened and a grey-haired officer came in—Buxton, standing-in this morning for Lemaitre, who had taken a week-end off. Buxton was a gentle man, who had never got higher than Chief Inspector's rank, was quite without ambition but as reliable as any.

"Good morning, sir."

"Hallo, Bux," Gideon greeted. "Know when Corbett dropped this note in?"

"Half an hour ago. He's over with Uniform now. Said he would look in later." Buxton went round to his desk. "Would you like me to call Hobbs in?"

"Please," said Gideon.

Hobbs was almost too short for a policeman, and probably topped the regulation 5 feet 8 inches—which Gideon secretly thought was too short—by only half an inch or so. He was Repton and King's College, Cambridge, and had spent a year on an exchange scholarship with an American university—for some quirk of a reason, Gideon could never remember whether it was Harvard, Yale or Princeton. There was something curiously controlled about Hobbs. His clothes were extremely well cut, but a shade on the snug side. His hair was always exactly the same—it never seemed too long or too short. He had a quiet manner, but the very quietness of it, allied to a voice which was more cultured than most men's at the Yard, made some of his colleagues feel that he was trying hard not to appear conscious of a superiority which he felt.

Gideon had a feeling that Hobbs was lonely here, and further that the impression of complete self-suffiency which he gave was wide of the mark. He seldom talked about his background or his private life. He was married but had no children. He lived in Chelsea, near the river—a perfect position for a Yard chief.

Most of the other seniors respected but did not like him. His aloofness certainly seemed like snobbery, as if he tolerated them without feeling one of them. There was no actual conflict, but Lemaitre, who had little tact, occasionally commented on the fact that Hobbs was getting more and more standoffish.

"Never has a drink across in the Row and never says a word more than he has to. Too bloody big for his boots, that's his trouble."

"Good morning, Commander," Hobbs said as he came in.

"Morning. Take a pew." Gideon waited until Hobbs was seated and asked: "What's new?"

He could not read Hobbs in the way that he could most of the others.

"I made a charge for the Soho murder early this morning," Hobbs reported. "It was the man we suspected. Middle-aged paranoiac. He's admitted it. Says he wanted her to give him some fancy stuff, and she wouldn't play, so he used the knife. I've been out to see his wife. She simply reiterated that she doesn't believe it, but—" Hobbs shrugged, and paused. He was speaking very quietly, almost as if he were reciting. "I don't think we shall have much difficulty, Commander. In fact the case is practically ready for the Public Prosecutor's office—if you'll give my recommendations and report consideration, I'll appreciate it."

He handed over a manilla folder.

"Monday do?" asked Gideon.

"Yes, of course."

"Right. Tired?"

Hobbs's face relaxed into one of his rare smiles.

"It hasn't exactly been exhausting, and I'm due for a week-end on duty."

Gideon grinned. "Your wife agree with that?"

An invisible barrier went up, and he realized that the moment he uttered the words "your wife." Was it because of domestic trouble, or was Hobbs determined to keep his work and his home separate? It was a tough thing for a policeman to attempt.

"I think so," Hobbs said.

"Good! Well, I want you to go over and see Colonel Tulson of the British Transport Commission. He'll probably take you to Sir Henry Corrington. They've both got an angle on some Transport police problems, and Parsons can't quite figure it out. I think you might be able to. Concentrate on it, will you, and let me know the minute you think you're getting close."

"I know Corrington slightly," Hobbs remarked, and the

barrier seemed to go down. "I'll get to it right away." He paused. "How is the Dean murder and the Wylie murder inquiry going?"

"No progress to speak of," Gideon replied. "We checked on the husband who deserted her, but he's in the clear. Any ideas about it?"

After a long pause, Hobbs said: "Yes, one."

"Let's have it."

"I may be sticking my neck out, but according to our present theories, the man known as Freckles killed the coloured girl to make sure she couldn't give him away as Dean's murderer. Mrs. Wylie lived in a street which is almost entirely taken over by coloured Jamaicans. I had a look down there myself yesterday, and I couldn't really understand how any white man—especially a conspicuous one with ginger hair and freckles—could get into a house along that street without being noticed. We've been concentrating on Freckles and the other, thickset white man. I wonder if we ought to be looking for a Jamaican, who could slip in and out of the street and houses more easily."

9

New Angles

THE possibility that they should be looking for a coloured man, other than the husband, had been teasing Gideon, but was an angle he had not yet discussed with Parsons or Boman. He wondered how long it had taken Hobbs to reach it. This wasn't a time to say that it had been in his mind: that would dampen enthusiasm.

"When did this occur to you?" he inquired.

"Yesterday morning."

Gideon said heavily: "Listen, Hobbs, it's the kind of angle we ought to be working on. If you sit on a thing like that for twenty-four hours, we might lose our murderer by the delay. If you get any more bright ideas about this or anything else, jot 'em down on a slip of paper for me—or give me a ring. Will you?"

"Sorry," said Hobbs, stiffly. "I didn't want to appear to be poaching."

"Only one job we've got to do, and that's get the swine," said Gideon. "If we start putting up hedges so as to keep off other people's ground we'll soon be in trouble." His hand slid into his pocket round the bowl of his pipe, and with the other he pushed the box of cigarettes across the desk.

Hobbs said: "Thanks." He took a cigarette and lit it with great care, watching Gideon even through the flame of a match.

"How are you finding it here?" Gideon asked.

Hobbs drew at the cigarette, as if considering closely.

"I wouldn't change places with anyone."

"That isn't quite what I meant."

"No," said Hobbs, and drew the smoke in so that he made hollows in his lean cheeks. "I didn't think it was. Taken by and large, I get along very well. There's much less prejudice than I expected."

He said that almost as if he were throwing down a gauntlet.

"Against the Old School Tie?"

"I suppose that's the basis of it," said Hobbs. "But I think you will find the hearty and the extrovert old school tie man getting along extremely well with most people here. I am not the extrovert type." He paused, but Gideon played the old game of possum, hoping that now he was launched Hobbs would really talk freely. Hobbs's lips twisted on the cigarette in a kind of droll smile, and when he did go on it was obviously very deliberately. "When I first came here, I didn't much like the other men, especially some of the seniors who were right at the top but who—"

He broke off, shrugging.

Gideon ventured: "Didn't study elocution?"

Hobbs's smile deepened.

"Yes, perhaps it was as superficial as accent and way of speaking. As a matter of fact, Commander, I've wanted to be a detective since I was a small boy. When others joined train spotter groups or collected stamps or went rock climbing, I read true life detective stories, and the memoirs of policemen, as well as text books. At the age of sixteen I knew Glaister backwards, and Gross on *Criminal Investigation* backwards and frontwards. Where the English literature addict was worshipping Shakespeare and Milton, the budding philosophers were revelling in Plato and Aristotle and the really serious minded were arguing over Freud and Jung, I was deep in Svensson-Wendel and Lombroso. They were like classics to me. Did you know King's allowed me to read Scientific Crime Detection as a special subject?"

"No."

"They did," said Hobbs, now fully launched. Gideon had the impression that he was really enjoying himself. "And I repaid them by learning the famous trials off by heart—I don't think there's one which I don't know, and I can almost imitate Birkett, Marshall Hall, Carson and the other great advocates. Then I went through the college, and came here. Most of the men I mixed with had hardly read of the figures I thought were the great ones in the field. I don't think I'll ever forget asking Lemaitre what he thought of Gross on *Hair*, and he said: 'Who's Gross?'."

Gideon didn't speak.

"All the other men seemed much the same, and while I was all for practical knowledge and the value of experience I thought that you could carry ignorance too far. It was a difficult period."

"Who did you tell about this?"

"No one," said Hobbs.

"No one at all?"

"No one." That barrier seemed to hover again, but slowly it was lowered. "Yes, it was what Lemaitre would call tough. The first time I began to feel better was when I heard him quoting chunks of Gross to a young sergeant—Lemaitre knew Gross as well as I did."

Gideon began to feel less troubled.

"Since this is a kind of confessional, I'd better tell you that was about the time when the practical technique of investigation preoccupied me less," Hobbs continued. "I could see exactly how it was done. As with the classics, I suppose, the great men of detection in the past learned the hard way, and what they learned came down to the moderns, who absorbed it without quite knowing where or how they'd learned what they knew. That was when I really began to enjoy the Yard."

He stopped; and was obviously determined to make Gideon comment. He stubbed out his cigarette, and helped himself to another; perhaps surprisingly, his fingers were trembling. The flame of his match trembled much more. Gideon took out his pipe and stuck it between his teeth, although it was empty.

"You got off the theory of the job on to the people who practise it, did you?"

Hobb's eyes lit up.

"That's exactly right, George, I—" he broke off. "Sorry." Gideon grinned.

"All right, Alec."

"Thanks," said Hobbs, quietly. "Thanks. I'm very glad I had a report to make this morning. You're usually so damned busy that it's a crime to take up your time. People who practise the theory of detection—yes. Until I began to see what went on in their minds, how they reacted—the professional crook and the once-in-a-lifetime offender, the sex criminal and the young delinquent—I didn't know much about people. I'm learning at last. I told you I wouldn't change places with anyone, and I meant it. I wouldn't go anywhere else, either. I made my own bed so far as Lemaitre and some of the others are concerned—they must have thought me a most stand-offish snob. I'll live through it."

"I don't doubt it," said Gideon drily. "Or rather, you'll work through it. There's nothing the men here like more than a good detective. They're the most single-minded lot you'll ever come across—anyone who hasn't a positive vocation for the job either falls by the way, or gets pushed into one of the other branches. Well! Glad we've had this talk. If there's anything you ever want to discuss with me—business or not—tell me. I'll make time. It might have to be one evening, or a week-end, but there is always time. Mind if I say one thing that might sound personal?"

Hobbs was smiling, perhaps a little warily.

"No."

Like all vocations, this is a full time job, waking, sleeping, day, night, in the office, on holiday, at home."

Hobbs said: "I think I know what you mean." He was silent for a moment. "Well, I'd better go and see if I can arrange a meeting with Tulson. You know what it's about, do you?"

"That's what you're going to see him for—to find out."

Hobbs said: "All right, George. Thanks." He nodded, stood up, and went to the door. He didn't look back as it closed on him. Gideon sat for a few seconds on his own, reflecting on everything that had been said, a little wry about the fact that he never appeared to have time for a senior officer, wondering whether there was in fact trouble at home, or whether Hobbs simply could not bring himself to discuss his wife and domestic affairs.

"Be interesting to find out," Gideon mused aloud, and a moment later his telephone bell rang three times in quick succession. The last caller was Boman.

"I got a message from you, George."

"Yes. Can you come over?" Gideon asked.

"Now?"

"Yes."

"What's new?"

"Come and find out," urged Gideon. He rang off, and a telephone rang again, one from outside—his direct line. He realized, without consciously thinking, that it might be Kate—occasionally she used this line if she wanted to talk about something that the Yard's operator couldn't overhear. It might be a newspaper man after a little off-the-record news, it could be Rogerson—who was also off for the week-end, but not far from London—or it could be a squeak.

"Gideon here."

He heard the sounds which meant the pennies were dropping into a prepayment box; so this was an outside call. Now his mind began to work faster. Most such calls came from informers.

"Mr. Gideon?" The speaker had the kind of voice which, in

his early days here, must have made Hobbs look down his nose.

"Yes?"

"You know me," the man said, in a whisper. "Nick Gadby, you know."

"What is it, Nick?" asked Gideon, in a friendly tone. It was a squeal, of course, but not necessarily important. He had his pencil in his hand.

"It's big, Mr. Gideon, really big," Gadby said. "How much is it worth?"

"How can I tell you before I know what it is?" asked Gideon. Gadby was a fringe man, a runner for a lot of professional thieves, and for fences, and he had never been known to squeal except on cases which were outside his own particular interest. Even with that there was a reservation: he had been used before now to squeal on a fence for the sake of another fence. There was no rigid criminal code of honour, although there was a code.

"Listen, Mr. Gideon." Gadby's voice seemed to become more husky. "I tell you it's reely big, it—"

"I haven't any time to waste," Gideon said brusquely. "What's it about?"

"Mr. Gideon," said Gadby, and now seemed to be breathing very hard, "how much would a line on that bus killer be worth? Eh?"

Gideon's fingers fastened round the thick pencil.

"If it's real news, I could spring fifty."

"Fifty!"

"That's our limit and you know it," said Gideon. "If I were you I'd take it quick—I don't want to have to send someone to pick you up." There was now nothing on his mind but this man and the hope he offered; Gadby would not have made this call unless he were sure of himself. "Let's have it."

There was a pause.

"If you try holding out on me—" Gideon began, and wondered if by chance he was going to be held up for more money: whether Gadby seriously believed that he could find much more than fifty pounds. Had he been wise to threaten? He didn't know this man well enough to be sure of his reactions to that kind of treatment.

"Gadby, if you—"

"Okay, Mr. Gideon," said Gadby, in a forlorn tone. "It's a bloody racket, though. Grinding down the faces of the poor, that's what it is. Well, you want to ask a few pertinent questions—ask a chap named Arty Gill where he was the night of Dean's murder *and* the night the bus conductress got hers. Arty Gill—lives on Hockley Lane, Bethnal Green. He's a garage mechanic, or so he calls himself, when he's working. Got that?"

"Yes," said Gideon, pencil moving fast. "What number Hockley Lane?"

"Don't ask me—halfway along, that's all I know—a few doors from the corner where the grocer's shop is. Mr. Gideon, how do I collect?"

"Where are you now?"

"I'm at Aldgate Station, by the bookstall. Mr. Gideon, I need the money quick, I don't mind telling you. If I could only get that money this afternoon it would be a godsend."

"Stand by the bookstall at Aldgate Station," said Gideon. "I'll have it sent over."

"Right away?"

"Right away," promised Gideon.

He rang off, and immediately lifted one of the other telephones. "Cashier," he said, and when a man in the cashier's office answered, he went on: "Gideon here. I'm going to send along for fifty pounds, in one pound notes and ten shilling notes—I'll make out the chit later. All right?" He waited for the assurance, and replaced the receiver, then lifted it again. "Sergeants' Room," he said, and while he waited he ran over the names of the sergeants on duty who were not known in the East End of London. A man answered. "This is Mr. Gideon," Gideon said. "Is Scott there?"

"Scott speaking, sir."

"Go along to the cashier's office, pick up a packet of money, and take it along to Aldgate East Station. You'll see a little man with a bald head and a glass eye standing by the bookstall. See that he gets the packet. His name is Gadby."

The man Scott sounded eager.

"Very good, sir!"

"Report to me as soon as you're back," ordered Gideon. He rang off, and immediately lifted the receiver again and asked for the NE Division, which covered Aldgate. It was a moment or two before he spoke to Christie, the Superintendent in charge. "Gideon," he announced. "Nick Gadby's just squealed on someone for the Dean job. I've sent a man to pay him off. Will you have him watched from Aldgate Station, so that we know where he goes and what he gets up to?"

"Right away," said Christie. "Think it's a false trail?"

"I just want to find out," Gideon answered. "There's another thing. Have you a pencil handy?"

"Yes."

"The squeal is that we want to question Arty Gill, of Hockley Lane, in your manor. He's a motor mechanic when he's working—maybe no more than a garage hand. Will you get some quick spadework done on Gill, without giving any cause for alarm?—we don't want to flush him before we're ready."

"Would happen at the week-end," Christie said. He was commenting, not complaining. "I'll fix it, George. I think old Walrus is on duty, he knows the Hockley Lane area as well as you know your square mile. You going to send someone over?"

"I'm coming over myself," Gideon told him. "I'll be in your office in about an hour. If there's any sign that Gill is going to cut and run for it, pick him up.

"Any charge?"

"Just for questioning."

"All right, George," Christie said. "I'll have a sandwich for you when you get here. Judging from the tone of your voice there isn't going to be much time for eating."

"I hope not," Gideon said.

Then, as he was about to ring off, one of the other telephones on his desk began to ring.

Paddy O'Neil, who had been so keenly interested at the Museum a few days earlier, stood on the platform of his Number 15 bus as it turned past Aldgate Pump, unaware of the fact that he was so near the window where Kenworthy frequently sat at the café. Paddy was whistling. Businessmen in bowlers, Cockney barrow boys with chokers and caps, office boys and office girls caught the bus or stepped off it.

"Next stop, the Bank of England!" Paddy called. No one took any notice, and he peered out at the pale mass of the Bank, at the columns of the Royal Exchange, at the other age-darkened commercial buildings and the seething mass of traffic. "Mansion House next," he shouted as he watched the doors of the Guildhall open, and someone go inside, wearing a top hat.

The bus stopped for traffic which was thick and tightly packed in each direction; at least twenty red double-deckers were in the jam, like Gullivers in a mechanical Lilliput. The stench of diesel and petrol fumes, the buzz, purr, clatter and roar of engines, the tap-tap-tap-tap of footsteps on the pavement, made a rhythmic cacophony.

A girl came hurrying from the pavement.

She was rather tall, curly haired, postcard pretty. Her eyes were a bright blue, she made up a little too much, especially at her eyes and lips. Her figure made Paddy's eyes widen, and Paddy whistled a silent "*Pheeeww!*" She carried a big canvas satchel. Running, her breasts bobbed up and down in time with her curly hair, and the satchel banged against her hips. She was heading for the bus, but as she drew within a few feet of it, it started off.

"Just take me hand, now!" Paddy called. He leaned out dangerously to help her. She stretched out and he caught her hand firmly—and the bus stopped again. Laughingly, the girl climbed on. Paddy let her go.

"Thank you ever so much!"

"I'm thinking it's one of the pleasures of me work," said Paddy.

She hitched the satchel round.

"Shall I pay now?"

"I'll be coming up to see you in a minute," Paddy told her. "Don't be in too much of a hurry to part with your money." He watched as she clambered up the steps, lovely legs soon on a level with his eyes, short skirt swirling. "Now, me boy," said Paddy aloud, and turned round.

An inspector hopped on the bus, and he recognized the guide at the Model Museum.

"Good morning, sorr."

"Morning. Don't help passengers on while the bus is moving, or you'll get yourself into trouble," the inspector said. "That's against the rules. Didn't you know?"

"Sure and I must have forgotten." Paddy was abashed.

"Well, remember it in future. May I see your machine?" Joe Ware checked the numbers on the printing machine which issued the tickets, and then went along on the inside.

"Two men and a girl are on top, I haven't collected their fares yet," said Paddy. "Is it all right if I go now?"

"Why not?" the inspector asked.

Paddy hurried up.

The girl had a seat at the front of the bus, and held a half crown on the palm of her hand. She held it out, turning round and smiling up at him. "Marble Arch, please."

"It's a long way you're going this morning."

"Any objection?" Her eyes laughed at him.

"None at all, me darlin', it's just an expression of me Irish curiosity."

Later on the journey, passing the Law Courts which look like parts of a mediaeval city, going round Trafalgar Square and watching the mass of people feeding the birds near the fountain, along Lower Regent Street to Piccadilly and the signs which flashed daylight defiance, along the handsome shops and regal crescent of Regent Street proper, and into Oxford Street, Paddy kept going up and having a word with the girl. He learned that she was a messenger for a firm of insurance brokers, and that she did a different route most days but it usually brought her to the Number 15.

"I'll be asking St. Patrick to make sure you find your way to my bus," said Paddy. "Good day to you."

He helped her off.

A man who had got on at Piccadilly, young, well-dressed, rather pale and with curiously shiny eyes, also stepped off the bus. Paddy was too interested in the girl to notice him, until he saw the man following the girl. The man eyed her up and down in a way which Paddy didn't like at all, but his bus swept him past.

He waved to the girl, and saw the man frown.

The young man watched the girl as she crossed to the Cumberland Hotel, but instead of following her, as he was tempted, he turned into Hyde Park, and walked along until he reached a parked car: a Jaguar sports model. He got in and sat at the wheel, and his eyes took on an even stranger brightness. He kept picturing that fair-haired girl as she walked along—bounced along rather—hair and bosom bobbing, skirts swirling above her knees. She had beautiful legs. She had everything. She was very like the last girl he had known.

The young man's name was George Cope.

His other name, a kind of *alias* known to millions, was the Seaside Strangler. No one but he knew it was his *alias*, but he often read about himself in the newspapers.

He certainly liked that girl.

After his ride on the Number 15 bus that day, old Joe Ware went back on a Number 23 to the Aldgate terminus to check some canteen and washroom arrangements. He remembered the little Irish conductor from the visit to the Museum, and hoped that he would not be too free with the girls. That was one tendency which could not be tolerated among the staff.

Joe left early in the afternoon, and was about to jump on a Number 5, which would take him into the heart of the crowded East End along Commercial Street, when another inspector came hurrying after him.

"Hey, Joe!"

Ware turned round.

"What's up, Sam?"

"Just had a nasty bit of business," the inspector answered. "One of our chaps has had his wallet pinched. The fool was crazy enough to leave it in his coat pocket when he was washing. You've been in the washroom, haven't you?"

"I was checking the clean towels and the soap containers," Ware said. "I didn't notice anything, but I'd better take full particulars. Told the police yet?"

"Our regular man's on holiday, someone's doing a shift. But Boman's sending a chap over. He wants us to take special notice of anything like this pinching. Is there much of it about, Joe?"

"A sight too much," replied Ware, rather gloomily.

He went inside to take particulars of the loss. He was still there when one of Boman's men arrived, and began to ask questions of everyone who had been in the bus station, but there were a lot of difficulties. For one thing, about a dozen bus crews had gone out between the time the victim of the theft had washed and the time he had missed his eleven pounds. Several relief drivers had been in, and several maintenance men including an electrician who had come to check some faults in the time clocks. In all, at least thirty people had come and gone during that period, and another twenty of the regular staff were about.

"And someone could have come in from the outside," remarked Joe Ward. "Don't forget that." He was back at the exit, with the depot man. "Had any Action Committee troubles here, Sam?"

"That damn commie, Higson, was here last week," replied Sam. "There's a lot of talk, but don't you fret, it won't come to anything. I'll let you know if there looks like being any trouble. We're too busy for that lark."

10

On The Run

SUDDENLY, Gideon was also too busy.

He had known that the slack period would end before long, but was not prepared for it to break on a Saturday morning, when the Yard was understaffed. He hesitated before lifting the telephone, wondering whether it would be a good idea to let Buxton take the message. Buxton was in the next door office, and would come at a moment's notice. Suddenly Gideon lifted the receiver, and with his other hand, pressed the bell for his stand-in assistant.

"Gideon here."

"Morning, George." It was Lemaitre. "Remember me?"

"I thought you were going off for the week-end."

"And I'm on my way," Lemaitre assured him. "But I forgot one little thing. Thought you'd better know so that you can brood over it this week-end. I know Kate couldn't stand it if you were mooning around all day. Those tube accidents."

"Yes?"

"I was making a graph of them, and some notes," said Lemaitre. "Three of them occurred near the exits at three stations which have exits near the front end of the trains. Did you spot that?"

"Something like it."

"Here's another coincidence," Lemaitre said. "One of this three was a chemist's assistant—worked in a shop in Hampstead. Another was a woman accountant at Chindini's, the big drug manufacturers—Boman made a note of what she did for a living, but not where she worked. I dug it out. And the third one was the wife of a doctor. All had something to do with drugs—see what I'm driving at?"

"Yes," said Gideon, heavily. "Pharmaceutical drugs."

"Lot of money in them, George." Lemaitre said blithely. "Had to make sure you weren't sitting and twiddling your thumbs. How are tricks? Nice and quiet?"

Gideon said: "There's a lot building up. Don't be late on Monday."

"No, teacher." Lemaitre laughed and rang off.

Gideon looked at the notes he had made. A pharmaceutical chemist's assistant, an accountant at a firm of wholesale manufacturing druggists, and a doctor's wife. He was tempted to turn up the files which Lemaitre had prepared and the others which Boman had brought in, but did not see that it would do much good. Instead, he called the operator. Corbett, who had reported the story of a man who had nearly been pushed under a train, was now in Parsons' office.

"This chap who says he was pushed off the tube platform at Piccadilly—" Gideon said.

"Nearly pushed off, George," Corbett answered.

"Yes. What's he doing for a living?"

"He's an accountant."

"Where?"

"Some big firm in the West End—manufacturing chemists, what's their name—Chindini & Company."

"Oh, is he?" said Gideon. "Keep a very close eye on him, will you? A woman in the Accounts Department at Chindini's actually died in front of a tube train some years ago."

"Well I'm damned," said Corbett. "Good job I didn't lose any time telling you about him. Thanks, George. How are things going this morning?"

"They're hotting up," Gideon said. "I'll probably be there this afternoon. If I'm not, I'll telephone you."

"Listen, George! I'm due to play bowls—"

"Who'll be in charge at LI?"

"Old Day."

"I'll talk to him if necessary," Gideon said. "Have a good match."

Corbett was a veteran bowls player, and mustard keen. There were times when Gideon himself wished that he had taken up golf, or bowls, or any recreation, game or hobby which would have given him a complete change from the daily grind, but in his younger days he had been too busy, and now there simply wasn't time to learn. He got to his feet, strolled over to the window, and gazed out over the Embankment and the river. It looked beautiful. Hundreds of people were sunbathing on the parapet of the Embankment, and at least a dozen gaily coloured awnings were floating gently along the smooth river—tripper boats packed to capacity. One half of the world didn't know—he broke off in the middle of the trite reflection, slipped into his coat, and then said: "*Blast it.*" One of the telephones rang.

At the same moment, Buxton came in.

"See who it is, will you?" asked Gideon. He watched the Embankment and saw a Rolls-Royce turn into the Yard gates. It was surprising that no one had warned him of such a V.I.P. visitor.

Buxton said: "Mrs. Gideon on the line, sir."

"Oh." It would be, the only time he hadn't answered the telephone himself. He strode across. "Hallo, Kate! I'm glad you called, because I don't think I'll be home this afternoon."

"Oh, what a pity," Kate said, without sounding very disturbed. "As a matter of fact, George, the girls have tickets for a matinee of *Oliver* this afternoon, and I was going to find out if you would be late."

He chuckled.

"If you can enjoy sitting and watching the stage on a day like this, off you go," he said. "I hope to be in about six." He was tempted to suggest that the family should meet somewhere in town for the evening meal, but checked himself. He wasn't sure what time he would be finished, and few things were more unsettling than failing to keep a family appointment; the years had taught him to be very careful about making them.

"Be back as soon as you can," Kate said. "There's some ham, or sausages if you prefer to cook them."

"I won't starve," Gideon assured her.

He rang off, rubbed his chin, and became aware of Buxton glancing up at him. Buxton had a funny habit of looking up from under his stubby, dark, lashes, so that he seemed almost furtive. Now, he peered up more frankly.

"Mr. Corbett's outside, sir."

"And Parsons?"

"Yes. They're together."

"So Corbett gave up his bowls," Gideon remarked. "O.K. We'll have 'em in."

It was obvious that the two men had already been in a huddle. Parsons had his pious, couldn't-do-anyone-any-harm look, which told of satisfaction and perhaps concealed eagerness. Corbett looked like his namesake of old, the great Jim of the bare knuckle days, and that was not really surprising. There was a story that he was a descendant of the old fighter, certainly he had won the Metropolitan Police Force's Heavyweight Boxing Championship four years running. That was a long time ago; in fact, some thirty years ago. He had a broken nose to show for it, and breathed rather heavily when relaxed—giving an occasional little snort. He called it sinus; in fact it was the result of misplaced gristle which should have been surgically removed many years earlier.

They shook hands.

"You've told Vic?" Gideon said.

"He wormed it out of me," Tim Corbett replied.

"I'd like to go over with Tim—" Parsons began.

"No luck," said Gideon, and immediately told them about the squeal from Nick Gadby. Parsons's eyes began to shine. There was nothing very parsonical about him as he stood waiting for the end of the story.

"We'll soon see that so-and-so strung up," he said.

"Can't say I'm sorry that it's not in my manor," said Corbett. "What about my story about the chap being pushed in front of the tube train?"

"Boman's on his way to see you at LI," said Gideon. "Remember him? He—"

"Don't be an ass. The London Transport Police H.Q. is out at Park Royal, Beau and me spend an evening together most weeks. Are you sending anyone from the Yard yet?"

"I think we'll let Boman have a chat with this man who thinks he was pushed—what's his name?"

"Delancy. Hildegard Delancy."

"Usually a girl's name," Gideon remarked. "HILDEGARD?" He was writing.

"Yes."

"We'll see what Boman makes of it," Gideon went on. "Any sign of resentment with him? That we're taking a hand, I mean."

"With Beau? Don't be daft."

Gideon laughed.

"George," said Parsons, speaking for the first time since his outburst.

"Yes?"

"I've just had an idea. It's no more than a glimmering, but—*could* there be any connection between the bus murder and the tube train deaths?"

Gideon did not reply at once, just stood there and rubbed his chin. It wasn't often that Parsons disappointed him, but this was sheer guesswork—unless he had something to go on which he hadn't yet divulged. Not only was it guesswork, but it was highly improbable. Even if it turned out to be true it would still be improbable. The murder of Robert Dean had been for thirty pounds. Hadn't it?

"Worth thinking about," he temporized. "I wouldn't like to put any money on it, at the moment."

"It's been nagging at me," Parsons said. "Just as well to get it off my mind. Want me to go out to NE Division?"

"Yes," said Gideon. "I'm coming over, too." Then he thought: He's got this new bee in his bonnet, why not let him get it out? "Unless you'd rather go over with Tim here, and meet Boman then go on with him to see this Hildegard Delancy. I don't want to overawe Delancy, mind you."

"I can be one of Boman's men," said Parsons, and gave a sanctimonious-seeming smile. "Beau will love that. Supposing I call you at home when I'm through."

"After I've finished at NE I'm coming back here," announced Gideon. "You're not playing golf or bowls or tiddleywinks this afternoon, are you?"

Parsons laughed.

Almost at that identical moment, Arty Gill laughed too.

He was at Chris's Garage, which stood between some of dockland's oldest wharves and warehouses, and Thames View Flats. The Flats, twelve stories high, comprised the tallest and most modern apartment buildings on that section of the river. From the higher floors one could see the Thames winding and looping in both directions, and St. Pauls, London Bridge, Tower Bridge, the Tower itself, the Houses of Parliament—most of the familiar landmarks. The big structures of the Flats, all built to the same design, all earning scowls and derision from those who preferred the old type of terrace house, were as modern inside as out.

Most of the people who lived in them had once lived in London's worst slums. What Nazi bombing hadn't demolished the Slum Clearance Scheme had, and now these bright shiny square buildings with their big windows and small balconies had risen out of the rubble.

Many of the tenants had cars, and Chris's garage also did a lot of business with the commercial users of the docks.

The name "Chris" had stuck from years ago, when a man named Christopher Dill had owned a little corrugated iron shack and a petrol pump selling petrol at 11*d.* a gallon. Now the place was as modern as the blocks of flats, with a concrete mushroom for a roof, a dozen bright and shining petrol pumps, and a dozen mechanics and attendants.

Arty Gill was one of the pump attendants, a job he often did at garages in the East End, especially as a part-time worker at rush-hours, or at week-ends and holidays.

He was laughing at his reflection in the mirror, in the toilet. The laughter was deep and almost convulsive, for the hair in front of him was so unfamiliar—as dark as Bert Symes's. Jet black! It was cut short, too; every tiny strand, every piece which overlapped one of his big ears, had gone. Provided he wore a cap, no one would be likely to notice his change of colour. *Ginger? Don't be daft, you're barmy!* He did not give a thought to his freckles. He ran a short-toothed comb through his hair slowly and carefully, handling the hair after the teeth went through it to make it nice and sleek. Every stroke put him in better humour. "*Ginger, you're barmy,*" he crooned. When at last he had finished, he took out a cigarette and lit it, the match cupped in both hands. He puffed smoke out, squared his shoulders, took a final look at his reflection, and said:

"Look out, you women. I'm coming!"

He opened the door, and peered out cautiously. The toilet was discreetly at the back of the cement mushroom, and he could be seen only from the top floors of one of the enormous blocks of flats. A girl was actually up there, hanging out some panties. She seemed to have little on. He winked to her, as if she could see him, and then waved. She darted back out of sight.

"See what I mean?" Arty Gill said to the world.

Two trucks, a motor scooter and a car were drawn up at the

pumps. One of the older attendants beckoned him, and was scowling. Bert was giving a lorry driver change. Gill went briskly to the waiting motor scooter.

"How much, mate?"

"Half a gallon."

"What's up? Going round the world?"

Gill laughed as he spoke, laughed as he pumped the petrol in, and was thoroughly pleased with himself. Since the newspaper descriptions, which had come unpleasantly close to him, he had been very much on edge. Bert had suggested dyeing his hair and putting on a different boiler suit from usual—one that flapped around him, much too big. It was hot, but who cared. *Ginger, you're barmy.* The reaction from tension was too great. A girl came up with another girl pillion rider, and Gill squeezed her hand when he gave her the change.

"Who'd you think you are, you slob?" she said, and pulled her hand free.

No one else seemed to notice.

As the day wore on, something of Arty's confidence faded, but he was still full of himself, and much happier than he had been for some time. With that conductress dead, no one could identify him for certain, that was the main thing. By the time lunch-hour approached—he went late, at half past one—there were times when he actually forgot the black hair and his fear for minutes on end.

When he left for lunch, Bert Symes was one of two men on duty, and Bert saw a big car draw up with two big men in it. He served ten gallons of mixture, took the money, and appeared to take no more notice of the car. As it disappeared round a corner, however, he lifted the telephone and dialled Kenworthy's home number.

Kenworthy answered at once.

"I think the cops are on to Arty," Symes said abruptly. "We've got to lay on something, quick. If they start questioning him, he'll squeal."

"But how—" Kenworthy began, in alarm.

"I've been thinking what to do in an emergency," Bert said. "That's why I said send him to this place. My sister lives . . ."

He talked in a low-pitched, urgent voice, and Kenworthy hardly questioned his authority.

When Arty Gill came back after his luncheon, something happened to scare him almost at once. A police car turned into the street. For a moment he was scared stiff. He would probably have turned and run out of sight, but for Bert Symes, who was close at his side.

"Go and take a dekko at that M.G., Arty. Hide your face."

Gill obeyed, but his nerves were jumping. The worst of it was, he could not see what was going on between Bert and the police. They were talking for a long time. At last he could stand it no longer, and glanced up and around. The police driver was letting in the clutch. He waited until the car had moved off, then hurried to Bert, who was holding a card in his hand.

"What did they want?"

"You," Bert said flatly.

"Now, listen. They couldn't—"

Bert's little unwinking eyes seemed to glitter. His hard, rock-like face hardly moved; even his lips hardly moved.

"You're Arthur Gill, ain't you?"

"*God!*"

"They want you all right," Bert said. His voice was unbelievably hard, like a sound out of a metal tube. "Ever seen this before?"

He held out the card. It was a photograph, obviously of a drawing or a cartoon, not a real face, but it was so like him that he almost cried out. The nose was too large and the ears too small, but the general appearance was unmistakable.

"How—how the hell did they get hold of that?"

"It's a composite picture, made by the Identikit system,"

Bert told him, carefully. "The police aren't so dumb. In fact they're damned clever. That's one of the things you've got to learn."

"What did you—did you tell them?"

"What do you think I told them?"

"Don't give me so much lip!" screeched Gill. "You're in this as much as I am—*you* killed that clippie, don't forget. Tell me what you said to the cops."

"Listen, Arty," Bert said softly, "you're losing your nerve. That's a bad thing. Kenworthy was saying only this morning that we've got to keep our nerve." He seemed to sneer at the sight of Gill dabbing at his sweating forehead. "I told them you were here most days but hadn't been in this morning. I looked round for you, and they did too—and your black hair was showing, wasn't it?"

"It—it's good," Gill muttered. "No one would recognize me."

"That's right," said Bert. "How'd you feel?"

"I'm all right." Gill squared his shoulders. "I'm fine." He glanced across the road to the wall of a rubber warehouse, and saw a big man strolling along, as if he had nothing to do. Big, well-dressed men did not usually stroll along here. He looked further along the street. Two men were sitting in an open sports car. Just sitting. Gill pulled at his collar, and the button broke.

"Take it easy," Bert said. "They're waiting for you to turn up, they're not coming here unless you do." For the first time, he smiled, a quick flash of white teeth against swarthy skin. "So you're okay."

"Don't I know it! Bert—"

"If anything goes wrong and you have to run for it, use this to scare the wits out of the cops." Bert produced a small automatic from his boiler suit pocket, and slipped it into Gill's. "If you have to run, go to Southend—the usual place. I'll see you all right."

Gill hesitated, then touched the automatic pistol. The feel of it seemed to give him confidence. He fondled it, out of sight—until another car drove up.

Gill's impulse was to move away, but Bert hissed: "*Serve them.*"

He kept his eyes averted as he went up.

"How much?"

"Six gallons," that driver said.

Gill glanced at him—and at the man next to him. He seemed to freeze. There wasn't any doubt about the passenger, it was the boss at Scotland Yard. Gideon. *Gideon.* So this was another police car, cops wouldn't come up for petrol unless they wanted to look around. He fixed the pump, and went to the back, unscrewing the petrol filler cap with trembling fingers. He didn't watch the petrol going in, but looked at the sports car and the man across the road who was now walking in the other direction, then glanced at Gideon's back.

He finished serving, and went round to the driving window.

"One pound eight and eightpence," he muttered.

Gideon seemed to be studying him closely. He'd like to put a bullet between those clear eyes. He snatched change out of his pocket, and handed it to the driver, then turned away, quickly. The car moved off. Gill was sweating so badly that moisture dropped off his forehead.

Bert came up.

"How—how did they get hold of my name?" Gill muttered. "Someone—someone must have told them."

"Don't be a bloody fool."

"Someone must have told them!"

"Listen, Arty," Bert said, in a softer voice than usual, "it's okay, I tell you. They're watching in case you come, they don't know you're here. If they did, they would have held you by now."

"How did they—?"

"Why don't you take a rest?" asked Bert. "Why don't you go round back, and then across to the flats? You'll be all right there. My sister's on the top floor, you know that. She'll give you a drink. You can stay there as long as you like."

"Can I?" Gill was eager. "Can I—?"

He broke off.

The sports car was moving slowly along the road. The man from the warehouse side was walking across—slowly. Another car, further along the street, was also crawling towards them. Arty gulped, turned, and half ran towards the toilet where a few hours before he had been so sure of himself. He waited there for a minute, fingering the gun, then peeped out; he could see no one. The walk from here to the wall which divided the garage from the block of flats was only a few seconds, and there were tall piles of old tyres to give him cover. He made a dash for it. He could not be sure whether he had been seen or not. He made a running jump at the wall and scrambled over—and as he leapt, he saw at least four men approaching, one of them inside the grounds of the apartments.

This man called: "Call it a day, Gill."

Gill said shrilly: "Get out of my way!"

"You're surrounded. You haven't got a chance." The man was still approaching, warily, and Gill heard a scrambling sound on the wall. More police were coming. He snatched the gun out of his pocket and pointed it at the man in front of him. He saw the flare of alarm before the man leapt at him, as if trying to catch him in a tackle. He squeezed the trigger. He heard the bark of the shot. He saw the man pitch forward. He saw the red splodge which appeared on the top of his head—just at the hair-line.

Someone behind him roared:

"Careful! He's got a gun."

11

Amok

THAT'S right, Gill thought in sudden frenzy, I've got a gun. He turned round. A plainclothes man was on top of the wall only a few yards away. He couldn't be missed. His face showed the same kind of fear as the first man's. Gill shot at him, but didn't wait to see whether he had scored a hit. He turned and raced towards one of the doorways of the flats. He knew them inside out, knew each floor, the lifts, the staircases. As he rushed into the first hallway, a door opened and a woman appeared, with a baby in her arms. She stood stock still, face blanching. Gill waved the gun, and she swayed back. He raced up the stairs. At the third flight a small boy appeared, sucking an ice-lolly. He did not even look frightened. Gill swept his arm round and sent him thumping against the wall.

Then Gill saw the lift, standing at this floor.

He dived into it, and pressed the twelfth floor button. The higher he could get, the further away he would be from the police. All he needed was somewhere to hide. The lift was slow. There were other lifts. None of them served this particluar part of the building, but all lifts went to the roof terrace; that was a danger.

What was he going to do?

He was gasping for breath when the lift stopped, and the door slid open. He started to step out, hesitated, then peered out in each direction. No one was in sight. He heard the blast of a police whistle outside—it seemed a long way off and gave him a momentary if false comfort. Each of these blocks was the same. On each floor there was a terrace which ran right round the outside, allowing room for exercise and for children's play pens. Each flat had one door—French window type—leading to the terrace. The main approach was from the halls, by the stairs and lifts.

Bert's sister lived four doors along from Gill. The safest way to reach her was via the terrace. At this time of day she was likely to be at home, her husband working at the docks, the three children at school. He sidled along a blank wall. Between him and his goal were two other flats and he had to pass the windows. As he crept along, he thought he heard the lift whining; next moment he thought he heard footsteps somewhere near. He whirled round.

No one was in sight.

He ducked past the two windows, and felt much safer, but now his mind was beginning to work more clearly. The truth was, he was trapped. All they had to do was to surround the block day and night—they could close up all exits. He began to sweat again, the brief comfort gone. His thoughts turned desperately this way and that. They would have to search every flat before they found him. They couldn't get a search warrant for *all* those places, could they? If he got into Ruth's, hid under a bed, even if she let them in—but all they would do would be to ask at the door, wouldn't it?

He was close to her door.

He was stepping toward it when he heard a whispering voice.

"*Arty.*"

He stood very still, looking round, heart thumping, breath hissing.

"*Arty!*"

It was Kenworthy's voice.

He couldn't see Kenworthy, who must be just round the corner.

"This way, Arty. The fire escape."

Gill heard a door slam, behind him; and at the same time looked across at the next block of flats, and saw policemen on the terrace. Suddenly a megaphone sounded, followed by a policeman's voice, hollow and resonant.

"Give yourself up, Gill. You're surrounded. You haven't got a chance. Give yourself up, like a sensible chap."

His fingers were very tight about the butt of the gun.

"Arty," came the whisper. *"Fire escape. Flat 173. You'll get help there. Fire escape."*

The voice was coming from Bert's sister's flat, one of the top windows was open. The megaphone voice was bawling again: what the hell did they think he was? He was tempted to shoot across at the men on the other terrace, and then warned himself that he must save his ammunition; he didn't know how much he would need.

"Okay," he whispered.

He saw the iron steps of the fire escape not far ahead of him, the little metal landing at the top of them protected by a gate to prevent children from climbing over, but he could just step over it. *Fire Escape. Flat 173—on the next floor, then.*

Heart pounding, lips stretched taut in a grin, gun in hand, he went forward.

Gideon was near the foot of the fire escape.

He had looked into Arty Gill's face, seen the freckles, and felt sure that it was the right man. He could have charged him, there and then, but taking Gill into custody was strictly speaking the Division's job, and he always liked to stand aside for the Divisions when he could—and when it would do no harm. He had heard of the situation by radio, and come straight here instead of going to Christie's office.

That Gill was dangerous, everyone knew; but there had been

nothing to suggest that he would use a gun—until that sudden shot, the cry which had followed it, the second shot. Gideon, approaching the building and looking upwards, had seen the second plainclothes man topple from the wall. He did not know for sure how either of the wounded men was, now; only that both were still alive. The apartment block was surrounded, the cellars were covered, there was no chance at all of Gill getting away, but—he had four more bullets at least.

A Divisional plainclothes man, tall, very lean, scowling, came towards him, followed by another.

"He's at the top, sir."

"Sure?"

"Yes—they've seen him from the next block."

"Which side?"

"This side."

"Right," said Gideon.

"Excuse me, sir—Mr. Christie's compliments."

"Yes?"

"He'll be along in a couple of minutes, sir. He'd like a word with you."

"I can imagine," Gideon said dryly. Christie was stalling of course, knowing that he would want to go up after Gill, and anxious that he shouldn't take any risks. "And he would like you to go up the fire escape, wouldn't he?"

"Yes, sir. We'll be all right. He—"

"Come up after me," Gideon said.

There was every excuse in the world for staying down here, and in some ways he knew that he should do. But there was more to this situation than plain common sense. The whole of this Division would know, by now, what was happening. The newspapers probably knew, and so the eyes of London were on him. He could, perhaps he *should,* stand aside. No one would blame him. No one would even hint that it was cowardly, and it would do no harm at all. On the other hand, it would do no good.

If he did go, however, and thus show every uniformed man

on the Force, every plainclothes man, everyone connected with the police that he did not think twice about going after an armed man, it would give the morale of the Force a tremendous boost. The fact that it would also get him a great deal of publicity was incidental. A few would say that it was showing off, but anyone who thought that wasn't worth considering. He knew exactly how sensitive the Force was, remembered from his old days what a fillip it was if one of the top men took a chance.

"Let me go first, sir." The gawky man actually tried to push past.

"That's enough," Gideon said. "One of you nip back to Mr. Christie, and tell him I think we ought to have a couple of automatics here—ask him to get permission, quick. I'll try to talk this lunatic out of shooting again. He might—"

There was a tremor on the rail of the fire escape, and he glanced up. It stretched way above his head, twelve flights up, a skeleton-like iron contraption, with only room for one person at a time. Between the treads he saw nothing but the yellow brick of the walls, the protruding window sills, the drain and stack pipes, and the sky. But that rail was quivering, as if someone was touching it.

Then he saw a man appear higher up.

He started to move upwards, cautiously. He was puzzled because he expected the man to look down, but the other didn't seem to be interested in anything happening down here. Instead, he dodged out of sight. The quivering continued, but was not so noticeable. Gideon quickened his pace. Anyone who was above him and on the escape must know that he was going up, and he wondered just what he would do if Gill appeared and pointed the gun downwards. It wasn't very likely. He would be much more likely to run, hoping to find another way down.

The man behind him said: "Careful, sir."

"I'll be careful," promised Gideon. "I'll dodge if—"

He broke off.

A man stepped on to the very edge of the fire escape. From

this angle, he looked all feet and legs, and it was impossible to tell whether it was Gill or not, but he was wearing a blue boiler suit, like Gill. Gideon was now halfway up. He saw the man peer over the side, and realized that the treads of the escape hid anyone down here from above; and made it impossible for anyone here to get a clear view of anyone up there. The man above might not even realize that the police were on the way up the fire escape.

The megaphone voice boomed: "Don't play the fool, Gill. Throw your gun down and give yourself up. Do you hear me? Throw your gun down."

There was no answering call. The fire escape quivered more, as if someone was treading on it heavily and hurriedly. Gill would want to rush down. The man must be a fool, or he would realize that all fire escapes were watched, like the lifts and internal staircases. A new thought struck Gideon: that Gill might be heading for a specific flat in this rabbit warren of apartments, might believe he could find a hide-out. If that were so, there wasn't much time. He went up the next flight quickly, hearing the breathing of the man behind him. He couldn't be more than three flights away from Gill.

Surely—

He heard a funny kind of screech.

There was a loud bang on the fire escape above his head, as if someone had fallen on it. The rail quivered, the metallic sound became a kind of booming echo.

Then Gideon saw a man toppling downwards, head first, arms waving, legs kicking. He was only a few yards above Gideon's head. His eyes were wide open, his mouth was wide open, in terror. For a split second, Gideon was almost paralyzed. Then it dawned on him that there was only one chance for the falling man. He leaned as far as he dared, pressing the railings, and stretched out both arms.

"Don't do it!" screeched the man behind him.

Gideon braced himself, felt the tendency to fall forward, realized what would happen if the full weight of that body did fall on his arms. Then he felt the Divisional man's arms loop round his waist, and at the same moment the body struck his outstretched hands. Its trajectory was away from the wall. There was a momentary weight on Gideon's hands, and one wrist bent back painfully; then the body dropped past.

Gideon was still leaning forward, not yet recovered, when it hit the concrete yard below.

Kenworthy, who had lured Arty Gill to the fire escape and the false promise of safety in the flat on a floor below, was in Bert's sister's flat; waiting fearfully. He had done what Bert had told him, knowing it was the only hope. But he hadn't expected the police to be so near. It was awful.

"Must have slipped," Christie said to Gideon. He looked rather like a colonel on parade, a brisk-speaking, brisk-moving, erect, square-shouldered man with close-cut hair and clipped moustache—every inch a soldier, although he had not been released for the Army.

"Slipped," said Gideon.

"Must have," Christie repeated. "As for you—George, when are you going to grow up?"

"What have I done now?"

"You could be on a stone slab."

"Well, I'm not. How are the men who were shot?"

Christie did not answer immediately, and that troubled Gideon. He waited, watching the NE man's alert, bright, sky-blue eyes.

They were on the top floor of the building, and half a dozen Divisional men were handling the routine, perhaps more thoroughly than seemed necessary. Christie was always excessively thorough, but the search now was for any evidence that a second man had been up here. Gideon had reported the man he had seen, but not yet explained his nebulous fears about that man.

Christie said: "One of our chaps will be all right in a week—a flesh wound. The other's not so good. Bullet in the head, and it could be fatal."

Gideon pursed his lips.

"He's at the Middlesex Hospital," Christie went on. "We should have some more news soon."

"Pass it on as soon as it comes."

"I will," promised Christie. "I sent Sarah Wallis over to see the man's wife and take her to the hospital." Sarah Wallis was the senior policewoman in his Division, and her compassion was a byword in the whole Metropolitan Force. "Well, we've got Gill. That's something."

"There were two men on that bus," Gideon remarked.

"We'll find the other, now." When Gideon made no answer, Christie went on: "Something on your mind?"

"Yes."

"Did he fall or was he pushed?"

"Yes."

"We didn't see anyone else up there, but there's a four-foot wall round each terrace, a man could hide behind it."

"It's possible he was tripped," Gideon said, rather ponderously. "And if he was pushed, it was to keep him quiet. Winifred Wylie was probably killed for the same reason. If Gill was pushed or tripped, we're really up against a devil."

Christie nodded.

"We want everyone at the garage questioned, and every flat searched," Gideon went on. "It won't make us popular but we can't pass it up. Can you manage without help from the Yard?"

"Just about," said Christie.

He reported to Gideon late that evening. According to the manager of the service station, Gill had worked for him as a relief hand, now and again. The other men at the station said they hardly knew Gill, although one, named Symes, admitted that he had seen him at various pubs and cafés. No one questioned in the flats admitted knowing him.

"The only one who seemed a bit edgy was a woman named Dale, who had a man-friend with her—her husband works on Saturday afternoon," Christie remarked. "Man friend *said* he'd called on business, but he was after a bit of dick all right."

There was no reason at all to doubt Christie's assessment of that situation; Gideon did not even know that the "man-friend" was named Kenworthy. Even if he had, it would have meant nothing at that time.

12

The Other Side

KENWORTHY sat at the window overlooking Aldgate Pump, again with an *Evening News* propped up in front of him. It was Monday afternoon. The Sunday newspapers had reported the death of Arty Gill in the most sensational manner. One had devoted a whole page of pictures to the shooting and the fall. Kenworthy had read every word, but not seen anything to suggest that the police suspected that Arty had been pushed.

The *Evening News* published interviews with people who lived in the block of flats, but there was nothing new. Kenworthy felt rather less on edge, but was not at all himself. He would never forget his terror when the police had called at Symes's sister's flat. She had brazened it out all right, and he had soon cottoned on. The police had been fooled, but he wouldn't like to go through anything like that again.

Ivy came to the door, and looked at him.

He knew that his wife was there but had no desire to turn and speak to her. He hoped she wouldn't start asking questions. She had been very quiet yesterday, making no comment about his moodiness, and she would probably keep that up.

Two things were worrying him.

The first, and the more urgent and immediate, was the

danger of being questioned about Arty's death, and the *murders* which Arty had committed. The newspapers, and presumably the police, had taken it for granted that Arty had killed both the man Dean and the bus conductress, and that was precisely what Kenworthy and Symes wanted. It looked all right, but there was still a risk, because Arty had so often come to the café to turn in his "takings", and the police might suspect that he had come for more than a cup of coffee or a meal.

They hadn't called, yet; there was good reason to hope that they never would.

Behind this lessening anxiety there was another, which loomed larger and more menacing whenever Kenworthy thought about it. He did not know what to make of Bert Symes. Until the death of Dean he had assumed that Arty was the more powerful and dangerous of the two. Now he knew that had been a mistake, and no matter how much he thought about it, he could not make Symes out. He knew that Symes had been questioned by the police, and had asked him to telephone if he were questioned again. There had been no message. The trouble was, he could not be sure that Symes—he had stopped thinking of him as Bert—would do what he was told.

Symes scared him. The way he gave orders . . .

Ivy still stood in the doorway, watching, and that began to exasperate him. Why didn't she leave him alone? She must know that he was thinking.

She moved forward.

"Jack—" she began.

The telephone bell cut across her words.

Kenworthy started, violently. The telephone was fastened to the wall, near the door—nearer to Ivy than to Kenworthy. He saw her move, and called out sharply.

"I'll get it."

He thought that she was going to defy him, and she actually moved a pace, but when she looked into his face, his expression seemed to stop her. He snatched off the receiver.

"Kay's Café," he announced. His mouth was dry. He heard

the sound of pennies dropping in a prepayment call box, and began to breathe heavily, for this was probably Symes.

"Jack," Symes said, in his clipped voice.

"Speaking."

"It's okay," Symes said.

"What—what's okay?"

"The cops are fooled all right. They were quicker off the ball than I thought they'd be at the station, but it's okay. No one's been back to question my sister."

"Are you—are you sure?" Kenworthy glanced at Ivy, who was still in the open doorway, watching him intently. What did she want to stick her nose in for? He waved her away.

"Wouldn't say it if I wasn't sure," Symes said. "Have a hundred nicker for me at five o'clock."

"*What?*"

"You heard," Symes said. "A hundred quid. I'll call for it at five sharp."

"Listen, you mustn't come here! You—"

Symes didn't speak again, but hung up.

Kenworthy was so shaken by the demand and by the fact that Symes was actually coming there, that he stood with the receiver in his hand for several seconds, before putting it on the hook. He took out a packet of cigarettes and lit one, shook the match out, and dropped it.

Ivy said: "Jack, what's up?"

He did not look at her.

"Nothing's up."

"Jack, I can tell—"

"Shut up, can't you? If I say nothing's the matter then nothing's the matter."

"Don't you talk to me like that!" Her voice rose as anger flared, and she stepped quickly toward him. "I don't know what kind of a mess you've got yourself into, but there's no excuse for talking to me as if I'm a slut."

He said tensely: "Shut up, can't you?"

"I won't shut up!" She stood in front of him, eyes blazing,

one hand raised and finger wagging, feet planted wide apart. "I want to know what's going on. I want to know—"

"I told you to shut up!"

"And I told you, I won't!"

He shouted: *"Shut up, you bitch!"*

She caught her breath, stood poised, then swept her arm round and struck Kenworthy on the side of the face so violently that it sent him staggering against the wall. He thudded against it. He drew in a squealing kind of breath, and the rage in his eyes was frightening. He steadied himself, swore, then went for her. She flung up her hands to save her face, but he struck them aside and slapped her on each cheek, hard, stinging blows, throwing her head first this way, then that. Each slap sounded sharp, loud and clear.

He stopped at last.

The water urn hissed and bubbled. Ivy Kenworthy's breathing was shrill and tinny. Kenworthy stood drawing deep breaths in through his mouth.

"When I tell you to shut up, you shut up," he said gaspingly. "And clear out of here. I've got someone coming to see me on important business. You clear out."

She didn't speak, but stood glaring. At first her cheeks were bloodless, but gradually the colour came back, and they were flushed, as if red hot. Her eyes glittered. Her lips worked. They stood facing each other, like animals.

"I told you to clear out!" Kenworthy said shrilly. "Do I have to throw you out?"

"You try," she managed to say. "You just try."

She turned into the kitchen, went in, gripped the side of the door, and slammed it. Kenworthy went across and turned the key in the lock, then stood outside the door, breathing very hard, still too angry to see anything clearly. There was a back staircase to the kitchen, she could go out that way. Symes would come in the front way, as he always did. *Symes.* Kenworthy was sweating, and his face and forehead and the back of his neck were both hot and cold. He wiped the moisture away, and when he lit a cigarette, his fingers made it damp and difficult to draw. He could imagine Symes's voice, cold, terse, authoritative, telling *him* what to do.

The next hour dragged so much that he could have screamed. To make it worse, he began to realize what he had done to Ivy, and remorse knawed at him. Remorse, and fear of what her reaction might be. She was no one's fool. She didn't need him for support—she ran the café without much help from him, most weeks. She might walk out on him. Nonsense, she would think of the kids. He kept moistening his lips. He wanted a drink—not tea or coffee but a whiskey. There was none in the place. He got up and began to walk around. As the seconds passed and it drew near half past four, he kept glancing at his watch. At first he had hated the thought of Symes coming, but now longed for him to come. To talk to *him* like that! He'd teach the young swine where to get off. He'd make him see who was boss. Anger quickening the paces with which he stalked about the empty café, he banged into the formica-topped tables, ignoring the pictures of girls and of ships stuck to the walls.

At a moment when he wasn't expecting it, he heard a sharp metallic sound behind him. He swung round, facing the kitchen door, which he had locked. It opened, on Bert Symes. He looked squat, thickset and very powerful, and for a moment, in the poor light from the door, it looked almost as if he were coloured.

"Trying to keep me out?" he demanded.

Kenworthy said weakly: "I expected you to come the other way."

"Shows what a fool you are."

"Don't you—?" began Kenworthy, then saw the way Symes's deepset eyes were staring. His voice rose. "Don't talk to me like that!"

"Come off it," Symes said. He walked forward, without closing the door behind him. "You got that hundred?"

Kenworthy had never been really frightened before, but this

youth frightened him. He stood against a table, the edge pressing lightly against the back of his thighs, and watched as Symes held his right hand out, rubbing thumb and finger together.

"Give," Symes ordered.

The big-head, who did he think he was?

"Ken," Symes said in a low-pitched but very hard voice, "I told you to give."

Kenworthy drew in a deep breath.

"Don't you come in here talking to me like that," he shrilled. "I'm not giving you anything—get that straight." The words were out, but gave him no confidence. The last words seemed to stick to the roof of his mouth, and squeak out. Symes took two steps forward, hand still outstretched; the sound of thumb and forefinger together was audible, now; a faint hissing. "You keep away from me," Kenworthy said shrilly. "I'm the boss around here. You do what you're told, see. Get out of here. I'll tell you when I've got another job for you."

He pressed harder against the table; it cut into his legs, but he was hardly aware of it.

"Get me?" He tried to shout, but those two words came out as a croak. "You've got plenty of trouble." He broke off. "You killed that girl, *and* you killed Dean. I didn't have anything to do with—"

"You didn't have anything to do with Arty's sad end, did you?" Bert sneered.

It was strangely like the moment before Ivy had struck Kenworthy across the face. The vital difference was that there was no rage in Symes's expression. His eyes glinted but did not blaze. His body was still.

"You and Arty killed that man, if you hadn't we wouldn't be in this mess. You get out of here, and stay out until I tell you—"

Symes moved, swift, sudden, cyclonic. Kenworthy sensed what was going to happen, it was as if he had known it from the beginning, but there was nothing he could do to stop it. He thrust up his hands defensively, as his wife had. Symes's fist smashed into his stomach, causing such agony that he gave a retching scream, and dropped his hands. Fists which seemed to be weighted with lead smacked in his face, against his nose, his jaw, his eyes. He staggered back helplessly, striking out weakly, once trying to kick. He came up against a table. It crashed beneath him, and he fell backwards. He banged his head against the wall, and strange lights seemed to stab through his eyes, strange noises filled his ears. He slid down the wall. He was gasping for breath, terrified in case he was hit again, but all was still. There was red in front of his eyes. Red. *Blood.* He licked his lips, and knew the taste of blood. He saw the tables, the chairs, the windows, the gay posters, and Symes's feet. He heard a sharp ting of a bell—the bell of the till. The takings were in that till—fifty pounds, at least.

He tried to get to his feet.

He dashed his hand across his eyes, and glanced down, and saw the blood on the back of his hand, but at least for the moment he could see more clearly. Symes was at the till, taking everything out. Three times he stuffed a handful of money into his trousers pocket. When he did so a fourth time, a few silver coins fell out and rolled along the oilcloth. He pushed two chinking fistfuls of silver in his jacket pocket, then turned round, his hands full of coins.

"Listen, you," he said. "If you squeal to the cops, if you say half a word to them, I'll fix you proper. I laid on a squeal to the cops about Arty, I made the fool dye his hair knowing everyone who knew him would notice. That's how careful I am, Ken old pal. The cops came quicker than I expected, but *you* pushed Arty, remember—I couldn't have, I was at the pumps. Don't try any funny stuff, or my sister will mention to the cops that you were hiding at her place. She'll say you scared her into letting you stay. Don't run away with the idea that you can stop me—no one can."

He broke off at last.

Kenworthy half closed his eyes; he felt as if he were going to faint.

"Do what I say and you'll be safe," Symes went on. "You can be useful, see. You can be useful to *me*. I'm not going to sit back and let you handle the situation in penny numbers. You've got to think big in this business, and that's what it is—big business. You can be useful, so I'll give you a chance. But keep away from the cops."

When Kenworthy didn't speak, Symes took a step forward. "I asked you a question."

"Yes," muttered Kenworthy. "I—I understand. I—"

"You'd better," sneered Symes. "Because here are some things you don't know. I can *prove* you've been taking money from Arty and me. I can *prove* you did a deal with me and Arty, to kill that bus girl. See? I can *prove* it." He slid his left hand into his pocket and drew out a box which fitted tightly inside. "Know what this is? It's a tape recorder. Like to hear what it says? Like to hear your own voice when you said the best thing to do was to bump that girl off? Like to hear—?"

"I won't squeal," Kenworthy promised, in a quivering voice. "I wouldn't think of it."

Symes said: "You can't win, Ken my boy, unless you do things my way. From now on, I take over. Got that?"

"Yes! Yes, okay!"

"Don't forget it," Symes ordered. "If you do what you're told, I'll see you right. I'll make sure you get your share of the dough, too. Here's the first instalment."

He tossed the handful of copper coins at Kenworthy. Kenworthy ducked wildly, but several coins struck him in the face and one caught him on the eye so painfully that his eye began to water. He dashed the tears away. When at last he could open his eyes fully, he saw the smear of tears and blood on the back of his hand, and beyond it, the empty café. Symes had gone without another word and without a sound.

"Oh God," Kenworthy muttered. "Oh God. Ivy. *Ivy!*"

But there was no one to hear him.

He hauled himself to his feet, and staggered across to a mirror which advertised cigarettes. He stared into it, and almost cried out, his face was such a pulpy mess.

"He—he must have used a knuckleduster," Kenworthy sobbed. "He must have."

He went wearily into the café kitchen, and ran water into a big plastic bowl.

Bus Conductor Paddy O'Neil was very thoughtful on that particular day.

The fair-haired girl, whose name he now knew was Peggy Blessington, had been on his bus for a short distance. They had chatted before she had got off at Charing Cross. The young man with the very shiny eyes, who dressed so well, had followed her off. He seemed to be able to travel wherever and whenever he liked. Paddy had a feeling that he was deliberately chasing the girl.

Now she was waiting at one of the bus stops outside Lyons' Corner House. People were already thronging into Charing Cross Station, although it was an hour or more to rush hour.

Peggy Blessington waved to Paddy as the bus swung into Pall Mall, but did not know whether he noticed her. She hitched her satchel round, as she often did, and waited for a few minutes until a Number 11 bus came up. She went upstairs, which she always preferred, and a man followed her. She had noticed him before, several times, but he had never spoken to her. She had a feeling that he was following her. She took the one vacant seat at the front of the deck.

She was nineteen, the only daughter of a couple who had married late. They lived at Beckenham, and from her earliest childhood she had loved riding on London buses—just like Gideon's children, and millions of others. Her affection had lasted much longer. As a matter of fact she had been one of the happiest, most excited children on a school visit to the *Bus & Tube Museum*. Occasionally she went back there, for the sight of the bus routes, the tubes and railways which made a kind of jigsaw puzzle of London, fascinated her.

When she had seen the job as messenger advertised, she had applied for it eagerly; the more she saw of London, the more she loved it. Her idea of bliss was still to sit on a bus and watch the passing scene, and she enjoyed it especially on some of the outlying stretches when the driver could put on a burst of speed.

Of all the routes, Number 11 was her favourite. Here the lumbering double-decker carried her along little narrow streets, and near slums, eventually to Victoria, and then suddenly into the magnificence of Parliament Square, the Houses of Parliament and Big Ben. And it was even more wonderful because no sooner was Parliament Square behind her than she could see the whole vista of Whitehall—*and* the short little street which ran down to Scotland Yard. She would make up dreams about the cars turning out of Scotland Yard, and the big men walking to and from it.

Today, going from Charing Cross to Victoria, she noticed the bright red uniforms of the mounted sentries on duty at the Horse Guards, and the crowds about them, saw how the men still doffed their hats at the Cenotaph, and saw a very big man walking away from Scotland Yard, one she recognized from photographs but whose name she didn't know.

Big Ben was chiming . . .

When she got off at Victoria Street she noticed that the young man with the shining eyes got off too. But still he did not speak to her.

At Victoria Station there was a bus depot, and wash-and-brush-up cloakrooms for the busmen. That particular day, Fred Dibben was in the area. He had spent the morning with some of the linesmen and drivers on the Underground, because there had been some complaints that line maintenance was slack. Dibben was given all the details, and had been told it was thought that it was due to the activities of a strong Action Committee.

"Whenever that chap Higson comes round, we have trouble," he had been told.

Dibben disliked Higson intensely.

He was thinking about this when he went to indulge his one great weakness—"a cuppa" at any time of the day or night—in the canteen. Then he went back to head office in nearby Westminster Broadway, and made his report. He had been in for half an hour when Boman, whom he had known for years, came up to his desk.

"Afternoon, Fred."

"Hallo, Beau. What's keeping you away from the bad men?"

"Were you down at Victoria Station this afternoon?"

"Yes, I was. What about it?" Dibben was always sharp when questioned.

"Some devil's been round the lockers. Forced half of them, and pinched watches, cash and rings. Must have got away with a couple of hundred poundsworth of bits and pieces. You didn't notice anyone hanging about the locker rooms, did you?"

"Can't say I did," said Dibben, frowning. "But I'll tell you who I did see in the canteen."

"Who?"

"Higson."

"I know what you think about Higson," said Boman, "but it wasn't him this time. He didn't go into the locker room, he was with someone else all the time. Not that I think he'd pinch anything. The Action Committees are hot on keeping within the law. You know that.

"It's what they *say*," Dibben conceded. "There's a lot of difference between saying and doing."

It was quite true that Higson had been with someone else all the time, at the Victoria Depot. But one of the electrical technicians—the man who had been so interested in the depots at the museum—had not.

Boman discovered this, and began to check whether this man had also been at other depots during the robberies. So many were being committed now that it was becoming worrying. And he knew that in a way Corrington was looking to him to make sure that serious trouble didn't develop.

That afternoon, Sir Henry Corrington sat behind his large flat-topped desk, its red leather giving off a slightly oily odour. The odour did not worry Corrington, but whenever the leather was cleaned like this his sleeves and his hands were inclined to stick to the surface, and that always irritated him. Outwardly, he showed no sign of this irritation. He was immaculate, relaxed and rather satisfied with himself, for this discussion was going much the way he wanted. The discussion was with Boman, on the one hand—obviously the least important of the three men with him—and with Freddy Tulson and a man he had met before, but who was very unlike any Scotland yard officer he had ever met.

Detective Superintendent Hobbs spoke his, Corrington's language—and Tulson's. Boman didn't. Boman supplied details and information, was seldom at a loss for any item required in the general discussion, was not really out of his depth, but quite satisfied with his place. Tulson, a man of sixty, with a lot of silvery grey hair and a ruddy complexion, would convey everything that was said to the Board and probably to the Ministry, and that would be bound to reflect well on him, Corrington. With luck, it would persuade the Board to do the obvious thing—take action against these trouble-makers in the depots before they became a serious threat.

To do this, the co-operation of Scotland Yard was needed, and Hobbs seemed just the right man to make sure of it.

"What you mean, then, is that you're aiming at one hundred per cent co-operation between the Board and labour. You've had one strike free year and don't see why there shouldn't be a long strike free period—if everyone will play their part, Eh?"

"That's it, precisely," said Corrington.

Boman opened his mouth, then closed it again.

"It might sound like aiming at the moon," remarked Hobbs, "but it's worth aiming at. I'm not sure what reaction there will be from Commander Gideon, but I think he'll probably see it your way.

"Gideon," Corrington echoed, dubiously. "Don't you think this might be discussed at a higher level?"

"With Assistant Commissioner Rogerson, you mean?"

"Yes."

Hobbs gave his rather reluctant smile. "If I were to go to Rogerson he would refer everything to Gideon before discussing it with the Commissioner."

"No doubt about that," Boman interpolated. "Gideon's the man we want on our side."

"I should have thought—" began Corrington, and then spread his hands over the desk. "But you know best, Superintendent. When will you discuss the matter with him?"

"First thing tomorrow morning."

"That's excellent. Do you know him well enough to anticipate his reaction?"

"I think he'll be entirely objective," Hobbs said.

"Is there anything we can do to influence him?"

"Influence *Gid*eon?" Boman interjected, half amused, half shocked.

Hobbs gave that rather tight smile again.

"I've arranged to spend the evening with Superintendent Boman," he said. "Before I talk to Gideon I shall be fully briefed—and if I can get enough evidence to convince Gideon that a lot of these political agitators are really breaking the law, he won't lose any time getting busy."

"We can be sure of that," Boman said.

Corrington nodded, as if satisfied. After a few more minutes of general conversation, he stood up, shook hands with Hobbs and Boman, and showed them to the door. Tulson, sitting back with his knees crossed, so that his right leg stuck up in the air, pulled at an ear lobe, and said:

"Useful man, Hobbs."

"I hope so, Freddy," said Corrington. "I wish it wasn't necessary to deal at this Gideon level, but we'll give it a run, anyhow."

"Got to," said Tulson. He uncrossed his legs, and stood up. "I'm with you, anyhow. Tell you one way we could look at it."

"Yes?"

"If Gideon and the Yard *won't* play, and if there is any trouble, the Board won't be able to blame us—I mean, blame you: I think I'll put the situation as you see it to the Ministry, and make it clear that you're relying on help from the Yard. Eh?"

"I'll be very grateful if you will," Corrington said, and added thoughtfully: "You know, a word in the Minister's ear, at this stage, might be a very good thing. If the Commissioner of Police were exerting a little pressure from above, and Hobbs exerting more from below, it might squeeze Gideon into the right frame of mind."

"Tell you this," Tulson volunteered. "The Minister will be at the Home Secretary's party tonight—the one for the American Ambassador. Aren't you and Moira coming?"

"Yes."

At half past six, when Corrington reached home, Moira was in the drawing-room, mixing a Manhattan. He heard the tinkle of ice in the glass as she whisked it round the jug. She put it down, and he went across and kissed her lightly.

"Hallo, dear. Had a pleasant day?"

"My day's been perfectly all right," said Moira. "How about yours?"

"Not bad, not too bad at all," declared Corrington. "I think things are shaping up. I'll tell you about it while we're changing for dinner."

* * *

At half past nine that evening, Alec Hobbs turned the key in the lock of the front door of his apartment in Chelsea. As he closed the door, he heard the sound of music, played very softly. He went quietly across the little hall, saw the pilot light of the electric stove in the kitchen was on, and smiled faintly as he went into the one big room of the flat. It was a combination of sitting-room, living-room and bedroom, which overlooked the Thames. Sitting up on silk cushions on a couch placed along-side the window, his wife had the radio on close to her side, books and magazines and newspapers handy, a tapestry rolled up on the window sill in a transparent bag which also contained different-coloured wools. Hobbs stood in the doorway, looking at her. She was gazing dreamily out over the river, and had not heard him come in. Her hands, so beautiful and yet so white, lay on the pale green spread which covered her.

She was the most beautiful woman Hobbs knew.

And she was one of the most helpless, for paralysis had robbed her legs of strength, and was creeping up towards her waist. She could still ease herself into a wheel chair, but every time she did so, it tired her.

"Hallo, Helen," he said.

She started, and looked at him. Her eyes glowed.

"The trouble is, I've never really put it to the test before," said Hildegard Delancy. "I told you last week, Em, I've not really had a girl, and I suppose it *is* a bit rough on my mother."

"I don't see why it's rough," Emily Smith remarked, but there was no strong feeling in her voice, and she smiled in the way which Delancy liked so much. They were sitting together behind some bushes on Ealing Common, within sound but not within sight of other people. A few pieces of yellowish grass were in Emily's hair, and one of her shoulder straps showed above the wide, square neck of her green dress. "After all, mothers know their sons are going to have girl friends, they can't expect to keep them for ever."

"Oh, she'll come round," said Delancy, confidently. "But when I told her I wasn't going to be home until late tonight, for the fourth night running—"

He broke off.

Emily leaned towards him.

"It's worth it, Gard, isn't it?"

"*Worth* it," he said chokily. "*Worth* it!"

It was a little while afterwards, when dusk was falling on that warm summer's night, and when many other couples were making their reluctant way homewards, arms intertwined, heads close together, that Emily asked:

"Did the police say anything else to you about Thursday night?"

"As a matter of fact, they didn't. They just asked me to say nothing else about it, and promised to make inquiries. I bet I know what that means. The case is closed!" Delancy laughed. "I've almost forgotten it now, except when I stand near the edge of the platform on the tube. It gives me the jitters."

"I'll always hold you," Emily promised. "It was funny about that woman, wasn't it?"

Delancy had told her about the woman in the accounts department of Chindini's who had fallen in front of a tube train some years before, and been killed. It had been an accident, of course, there wasn't any doubt about that, but it was a coincidence. Just now, under the darkening sky, all he could think about was Emily, and the immediate problem of the trouble with his mother.

He wished he had not told Emily about that woman.

He also wished he hadn't told his mother about Emily. She would be tight-lipped and difficult tonight, he was sure of that. And the last thing he wanted was to hurt her.

He took Emily home, and they spent five minutes in the porch of her house, hidden by a big privet hedge. Then Delancy made himself walk away, his lips still smarting from the passion of her kiss, his hand still aware of her soft, silky flesh. He walked quickly, almost blindly, and for a moment gaily. When he got to Hounslow East station it would be time enough to worry about coping with his mother.

He stepped into the road, opposite South Ealing Station.

A car seemed to roar and leap at him when he was halfway across, and in one terrible, terrifying moment, he thought that the end had come.

13
Gideon Annoyed

GIDEON turned into the courtyard of the Yard, on the Tuesday morning, after a slow and exasperating drive. Every stinking diesel truck in London seemed to have selected the Embankment, and he was thoroughly out of temper.

Word of this sped from the men on the gate to the men in the hall, and from there to Lemaitre, and to the sergeants and the inspectors. This morning Gideon had been frowning, the report ran, and had turned the wheel into the Yard more sharply than usual. He had nodded brusquely to the men on duty, so—look out.

Gideon knew the kind of warnings which preceded him, and more often than not it amused him, but there were times when it exasperated, and this was one. He lef this car parked very close to Rogerson's; the fact that Rogerson was in before him was also annoying. He was in the mood where he almost resented the fact that Kate hadn't got up to get him off, but he did not consciously think of that. He nodded to the sergeant in the hall, and to a girl clerk and two inspectors in the big, slow-moving lift—why was it *nothing* would happen quickly this morning? He strode along the passage to his office, head thrust forward on his short, thick neck, shoulders seeming rather more rounded than usually, footsteps a little quicker. The door of the office was ajar, and when he got in he found the office empty, but Lemaitre's coat was on its hanger.

Lemaitre should know better than to go out leaving the door open—*and* leaving the office empty. If he were going to be away for more than a minute, he should have sent for Buxton. Gideon turned to his desk, and a gust of wind from the wide open window sent two sheets of paper fluttering.

He grabbed at one, and caught it before it reached the floor; that helped to mollify him a little. Then his telephone bell and one on Lemaitre's desk rang simultaneously. He picked up his own, with the other still ringing, and stood against the side of the desk.

"Gideon."

"George, come in as soon as you can, will you?" It was Rogerson.

"How urgent is it?" Gideon wanted to know.

"I've got to see the Commissioner at ten o'clock, and need some briefing on these bus and tube jobs."

It was now half past nine.

"Five minutes," Gideon said, and rang off. As he did so the door opened wide and Lemaitre rushed in, snatched off his receiver, and flicked a finger in greeting at the same time.

"Hi, George," he whispered, and bellowed into the mouthpiece. "Superintendent *Lee-mate-trer.*" He winked at Gideon, and on that instant Gideon felt better. Lemaitre was quite sure that he knew exactly how to handle "old Gee-Gee" and Lemaitre was probably quite right.

Gideon did not take his coat off or round his desk, but looked at the pile of reports, and told himself that he was going to have a heavy morning; the slack period seemed to have gone for good.

"Righty-ho!" Lemaitre banged the receiver down. "Morning, George, what a bloody morning. Everything's gone wrong. Buxton's not in, his wife says he's got a temperature—this summer flu, I expect—dunno how it is that everyone gets it except you and me. Talk about the balance of nature. The A.C.'s been on for you three times, he wants—"

"I've just talked to him"

"Rather you than me. Your old pal Hobbs has put in a special request for a long interview, and I told him it had better be after eleven thirty. So he made it for eleven thirty. Parsons was going to be here at ten, but he's dashed out to Ll. Corbett called him. Something to do with that Delancy chap with the girl's name.

Gideon raised his eyebrows.

"More trouble with him?"

"Seems like. Then about those old tube accidents, George—oh, damn and blast these telephones." He snatched one up. "Lemaitre—"

He broke off, and for a moment only anxiety showed in his expression. This was followed by an expression of such relief that Gideon felt his heart beating faster.

Lemaitre put the receiver down gently.

"That was the Middlesex Hospital. Christie's copper—you know, the one shot in the head—is off the danger list."

Gideon's heart gave a sudden lurch. The bad mood and all sense of irritation were stilled.

"That's a relief," he said. "Pass the word around. I'll be back as soon as I can. Tell all the other chaps that Gee-Gee's back to normal, too."

Lemaitre gaped.

"Anything else?" demanded Gideon.

"Don't—don't think so."

"Find out, or I'll get bad-tempered again."

Gideon flicked a finger at Lemaitre, and went out, now in full good humour. By the time he reached Rogerson's door he was thinking only of the news about Hildegard Delancy, and wondering what it was all about.

Miss Timson, Rogerson's secretary, smiled up from her desk at Gideon as he went in. She was a woman of forty-five or so, always dressed in blouse and skirt, beautifully turned out, beautifully groomed in every way. Somewhere in the background of her life there was an *affaire* with an Australian police inspector, and Gideon would not be surprised at any time to find that she had decided to emigrate so as to get married, but for the time being she was as efficient as a secretary could be, hardly recognizable as the sharp-voiced, tart busybody whom Gideon had once known.

"Is he free?" asked Gideon.

"Yes—he's expecting you, Commander." Miss Timson got up and opened the door, announced: "Mr. Gideon," and stood aside. As the door closed, Rogerson looked up from his desk, smiling. Gideon thought that he looked tired; there were times when he felt that Rogerson would not last much longer at full working pressure. Rogerson's lips were a little too blueish for reassurance.

"Morning, George. Sorry to push you."

"Can't be helped," said Gideon, and sat down as Rogerson waved to a chair. "What's on the Old Man's mind?"

"He's had some kind of a session last night with the Home Secretary and the Minister of Transport," Rogerson reported. "I don't know much about it yet, but he wants briefing on the bus murders, and everything we do in co-operation with the London Transport Police. Wouldn't like to talk to him yourself, would you?"

"How urgent is it?"

"All I know is that I've the weekly conference of Assistant Commissioners at ten o'clock, and I've got to be briefed by then. I can suggest that you go and see him later."

"See how things go, will you." asked Gideon. He sat back, filling the chair; frowning. "Home Secretary and Minister of Transport, eh? Not putting political pressure on him, are they?"

"If they are, he'll tell 'em where to get off."

"I should hope so," Gideon said, broodingly. After a moment, he straightened up: "Well, here's the present position . . ."

He talked for twenty minutes, knowing that there was very little which Rogerson would forget, and confident that by the end of the morning Sir Reginald Scott-Marle, the Commissioner of the Metropolitan Police, would be fully informed—even to the suspicion that Arty Gill had been murdered, and to the possibility that Hildegard Delancy had been the victim of attempted murder.

Rogerson glanced at his watch.

"Just right, George. Thanks. Got much in this morning?"

"You know about everything, I think. The only new thing is . . ." Gideon reported the accident to Delancy, before going out.

In the office, Lemaitre was sitting in his shirt-sleeves but looking almost as spick and span as Miss Timson. Today he had selected a pale-green shirt and a brown and green bow tie, in stripes. He was on the telephone, and cocked a thumb to Gideon, an "all's well" signal. Gideon took off his own coat, stood by the window for a minute, looking out, and watching the sunlight sparkle on the river. It was going to be very warm, the breeze had died down already. He thought, fleetingly: "I could do with a few days off. Do Kate good, too." Then he sat at his desk.

Lemaitre put his receiver down, but did not speak to Gideon, who began to look through the accumulation of reports. Many things had ganged up on him. To make matters worse, there had been five major crimes over the week-end: two Post Office raids, one bank vault robbery, the theft of Old Masters from a private collection, and the death of a valuable race-horse with clear indications of poisoning. For the next half hour he studied reports and talked to the men in charge of the new cases.

He sat back at last, and stretched.

"Who's next, Lem?"

"Hobbs made an arrest on that prostitute murder job, that's all over bar the shouting," Lemaitre said. "I told him not to worry about seeing you today, he'll just put in a report.

Ringall's down at Southend, after the Seaside Strangler. Hopes to find another bus ticket, after two months!"

Gideon frowned.

"Haven't we got any line at all on the chap yet?"

"No," said Lemaitre, as if surprised. "He could be the one who gets away."

"That's what I'm afraid of," said Gideon. "He's killed three girls in a row, and probably won't stop at that. Think Ringall's working fast enough on it?"

"He'd hate it if you told him he wasn't." Lemaitre sat back in his chair. "What he needs is a break, George."

"So does the next girl on that Strangler's list," Gideon said.

George Cope, the Seaside Strangler, was twenty-three. He had a pleasant manner, was quite good-looking, and had plenty of money. For many years he had found it easy to find girls who would sleep with him. He invariably chose a girl from what he considered an inferior social stratum, and made full play with his pretended public school background. He preferred girls with big breasts and small waists, and wasn't too concerned about their looks, other than that.

It was five weeks since he had been down to Southend, for a week-end with a girl. Far too long! The girl now on this bus had the right shape, and she even had a pretty face.

Although he had often travelled with her, deliberately, he did not know her name. He did know that she was a messenger for some City firm, for she always carried parcels and letters in a big satchel. He had occasionally watched her go into offices and come out within a few minutes—obviously she had delivered something to the place.

She often travelled on the Number 15 bus, as often on the Number 11. He liked the Number 15, which went nearer to his house, and made most of his pick-ups on the route. Girls seemed to trust a man they saw often on the same bus.

This girl sat on the seat opposite him, looking very fresh and gay this morning, a little too heavily made up. There wasn't any doubt about her nice legs and full figure—exactly the kind the Seaside Strangler liked to get to know. She wouldn't be *easy*. If she had been, she would have tried to get off with him by now, and at least found an excuse to talk.

She was almost shy; a lot of girls who used too much make-up *were* shy. Many were virgins, too. It might take some doing to persuade her to spend a week-end with him—but there was no fun in the easy conquest any more.

He shifted across his seat, and leaned toward her.

"I hope you won't think I've got a nerve, but I've often noticed you," he said. "May I come and sit next to you?"

His smile was so open and frank.

"Well, the seat's empty," she said.

As he joined her, the bus turned left, out of Regent Street into Oxford Street, and it thrust his body against hers. He had known that it would.

"My name's Cope," he said. "George Cope."

"I'm Peggy Blessington," she told him.

As she said that, Paddy O'Neil came clattering to the top deck, calling:

"Any more fares, if you please," in his strong Irish brogue. He saw the man and the girl talking, and his blue eyes clouded. He began to collect the fares, making pleasant remarks as he always did: "*Now could ye have a better day, sorr?*" "*Now why would it be any trouble to change a pound note?*"

The girl glanced up at him and smiled.

Gideon spent ten minutes concentrating on all the details of the Seaside Strangler cases, but came up with no fresh ideas. Ringall was certainly digging out facts, even if slowly, and he, Gideon, was probably too impatient. As he turned to the next file, the door opened and Lemaitre looked in. Parsons followed.

"Spare a minute, George?"

Gideon said: "Come in." He put Ringall and the Seaside

Strangler out of his mind as he studied Parsons. He felt sure that there was a lot on the man's mind, there was an impression of intensity more than eagerness, a bedside more than a pulpit manner. "What's this about more trouble with the man Delancy?"

Parsons said: "Knocked down and could have been killed by a car last night."

Gideon sat very still.

"*What?*" squawked Lemaitre.

"It's a fact," said Parsons. "A hit and run driver, too. Delancy got away with a shaking and concussion, but eyewitnesses say it was touch and go. He managed to jump nearly clear. The car bumper caught his trousers and ripped them off him, and he was flung into the kerb—a bus missed him by inches, too."

"What about the car?" demanded Gideon.

"Ford Zephyr. Black."

Gideon said: "How is Delancy now?"

"They took him to hospital, but he was well enough to go home. He's home now. He was out with a girl friend—the Emily Smith who saved him from the tube train. He took her home, and walked to the station. I'd say he was a bit starry-eyed, and didn't look too closely where he was going. But these eye-witnesses say that the car roared at him—almost as if the driver meant to knock him down."

"What does Delancy say?"

"He was too frightened to remember much about it."

"Yes," said Gideon. "Well, if someone tried to push him in front of that train and someone tried to kill him by car, we don't need telling he's really in trouble. How about the earlier tube cases? Any connection between them?"

"There isn't any doubt about a connection," declared Parsons. "They all seem to have a tie-up with Chindini's." He had been holding this item of news in reserve, and now leaned forward in his eagerness to get full value out of it. "One accountant at Chindini's West End offices. The chemist's assistant who died had been in Chindini's research laboratory for years before leaving. The doctor's wife was once a laboratory assistant at Chindini's big manufacturing plant, out at Croydon. What we need is someone inside at Chindini's. There's something funny going on there."

Gideon said slowly, thoughtfully: "We ought to have picked up that association before." It was partly his fault; the truth was that no one had seriously thought of wilful murder, only of suicide—and the police seldom delved deep into suicides, unless there were indications of foul play. He rubbed his chin. "We need a list of the board of directors of the firm, and a list of the chief executives and administrative heads. There must be one of them we can talk to about this. Having Delancy's house watched?"

"Yes."

"We'd better not lose sight of him," Gideon said, and as Parsons got up, he went on: "I keep wondering if there's anything to support that idea of yours about an association between the tube murders and the trouble on the buses."

"Doubt it," answered Parsons. "The more I think of it the less likely that seems. I was too close to it, and rationalized a guess. Anything more come in from Christie about Arty Gill?"

"Not yet."

"No trace of that other man you saw at the fire escape?"

"No. I'm expecting a report from Christie some time today. You'd better stay in charge of each job, as they overlap so much."

"Pleasure," said Parsons.

Gideon watched the door close behind him, then stared down at a closed file on his desk. He was picturing that second man he had seen on the fire escape just before Gill had fallen to his death. He had little doubt that the man had been looking for something, and had been moving stealthily, as little doubt that he had tripped Gill and sent him crashing. Yet if Lemaitre or Parsons or anyone else had suggested it on such flimsy evidence, he would have made them think again. He found himself smoothing the bowl of his pipe, he was so preoccupied.

Lemaitre joked: "Awake, George?"

Gideon glanced up.

"Sorry," said Lemaitre, perceptively. "Hugh Christie wants you. I wouldn't let him come through until you'd cleared everything else off your desk. Corrington's in the queue, too."

"Get Christie on the line," Gideon ordered. He waited until Lemaitre talked to Christie on an extension to one of the telephones on his desk, then picked up the receiver. He half wished that he could have postponed this talk for an hour or two, while everything else settled in his mind. "Hallo, Hugh," he said. "Glad about your copper. What's on?"

"A queer turn up," Christie said. "About the same case. Don't know whether I told you that we've found out that Arty Gill often used to go to a café in Aldgate. We were checking just as routine, to find out if he had any friends there who might tell us a bit more about his movements. The place is owned by a Mrs. Kenworthy. Her husband's been very badly beaten up lately, while she's walked out on him. Also, he was in one of the flats near the petrol station—the chap I told you about. The gentleman has a record, I'm told—petty larceny."

"Oh," said Gideon, softly. "Why did the wife walk out?"

"Someone in an office above the café said they heard a furious quarrel. Then Mrs. K.—Christian name Ivy—took off. That was yesterday afternoon. She hasn't shown up this morning, the café's kept going by the cook, a kitchen hand and two waitresses. Kenworthy's not been there either, but that's not unusual in the mornings. What is unusual is that his wife left their home in Whitechapel, and took the two kids—that was five o'clock yesterday afternoon, according to neighbours. Kenworthy got home about six, his face messed up. I had one of our chaps go round to see him this morning on the pretext of checking for a gas leak. He reports that Kenworthy had a bad bashing, probably with a knuckleduster, but he hasn't had any professional attention. The cuts are still raw. He *says* he had an accident on his motor cycle."

"Talked to the woman who gave him his alibi?"

"She says she can have a friend in if she wants to."

"Seen Kenworthy's wife?"

"Not yet. She's at her Mum's."

"Try her soon," Gideon urged.

Lemaitre promised that he would make the arrangements, and Gideon pulled the thin file marked "*Col. Tulson*" nearer, and opened it. Beyond the note that Tulson had wanted to talk to a Yard man, and the rather vague reference to agitators and strike-makers at various bus and train depots, there was nothing. Gideon pressed a bell, and a messenger appeared. Gideon said: "Send Mr. Hobbs in." He frowned as the door closed, for he was teased by something which had nothing to do with Hobbs or Tulson, but was rather like a word on the tip of the tongue. He realized, vaguely, that it was something he thought it worth discussing with Christie out at NE—about Arty Gill. He made a circle, put a question mark inside it, and the words "Arty G." above it, and then the door opened, and Hobbs came in. This morning, he was in navy blue, and looked appropriately dressed for a board meeting rather than for detective work.

"Good morning, Alec. Sorry I had to keep you."

"Good morning." Gideon noticed that Hobbs did not say "George." "It gave me more time to think things over."

"Sit down. Need a lot of thought, do they?"

Hobbs gave his restrained smile.

"I'm not sure that you will think so," he said. "May I be really frank?"

"Franker the better. It saves time."

"I also see it that way," said Hobbs, hitching up his trousers as he sat down; the crease was knife-edge. "I spent some time on Sunday with Colonel Tulson and with Sir Henry Corrington, and had cocktails with the Corringtons before dinner." By then it must have been obvious to Hobbs that Corrington really wanted something badly, Gideon thought. He remembered the summons to Rogerson's office, and the

Commissioner's consultations with the Home Secretary and the Minister of Transport. "And I spent most of yesterday afternoon at Sir Henry's office, with Tulson and Boman."

"Know what they're after?"

"Apparently Boman's men have done a very good job of keeping their ears open at the various depots, and apparently at each depot there is a small group, calling itself an Action Committee. These committees are continually making complaints about conditions, about food at the canteens, working schedules, and the like. According to Boman, they are working towards making sudden demands at all the depots simultaneously—demands which are almost sure to be rejected by the London Transport Executive."

Hobbs paused: Gideon nodded.

"Boman and the man who have been on the look-out for this kind of thing say they think the situation is hotting up. It wouldn't surprise them if the demands aren't made sometime in the next week or two. They don't yet know what the key demand will be—that's been kept very secret. They think it will be something which will enlist the sympathy of the rank-and-file, so that a call for an unofficial strike at any one depot is likely to be answered."

Gideon was sitting very still. "Yes?"

"Corrington believes—or says that he believes—that the London Transport Police can't do any more than this. That they've already gone as far as they dare, and that if their chaps dig any more deeply into the affairs of the Action Committees, then that in itself could become a grievance. It would be said that the police are going outside their proper terms of reference by taking political action. So Corrington would like us to assign at least one man to every depot of both buses and trains." Hobbs sat a little further back in his chair. "At least one man at each," he repeated, as if to make sure that Gideon understood.

Gideon said: "Oh, does he?" He no longer doubted that the pressure from the Home Office and the Ministry of Transport had to do with this. Corrington was pulling all the strings he could. Gideon did not yet feel any strong emotional reaction. He did not think that he knew enough about the situation yet, although he knew the principles involved only too well. After a long pause, he sat back in his chair, held the arms firmly in his big hands, and asked:

"What do you make of it?"

"Do you mean, what would I do in these circumstances?"

"Yes."

"I would ask Boman—or even Corrington himself—for any specific evidence that crimes are being committed in these depots. If there's any evidence I'd assign men to investigate. If there isn't, I wouldn't touch it." After a pause, Hobbs went on: "Would you, George?"

"That "George" meant a great deal.

Gideon leaned back, so that it looked as if his weight would break the back of the chair.

"We'd be justified in trying to find out if there is any form of conspiracy, I think. What did you make of Corrington?"

Hobbs looked surprised. "Well, I know him, of course. We were at—"

"I mean, his motives over this job."

"I see," said Hobbs, and hesitated. Then he gave his most relaxed smile. "He's completely sincere, I'm sure. He wants labour relations throughout the London Transport Board area to remain good, and knowing him well, I imagine that he thinks this will serve him in very good stead. He's an ambitious man. He knows that it's got beyond him and London Transport Police, and he doesn't like anything which gets beyond his control. Morally speaking, Henry Corrington believes that almost any means are justified if the end is right."

After a long pause, Gideon asked: "Do you?"

14

Police Visit

HOBBS sat very still, drawing softly at his cigarette, his gaze thoughtful and steady. He seemed to realize that this was a time of testing. Gideon had a chance to study his face closely. The good, smooth forehead with the dark hair receding, and brushed back very straight; the widow's peak—I wonder what the situation *is* between him and his wife, Gideon thought—the sharply defined eyebrows, the rather close-set eyes, dark blue and very clear, the slightly hooked nose, the thin lips and long chin, with a slight cleft. He had never really studied this man before.

"No," Hobbs answered him. "I don't believe that the end justifies the means, but sometimes I act as though I do."

"Ah," said Gideon.

"To get at the truth, I will lie to a suspect so as to trap him into an admission," Hobbs went on. "I will stretch the evidence further than I should in order to justify an arrest. I will go outside the letter of the law to scare a witness whom I think is lying. It's a conflict between philosophical theory and practice, and I suppose the truth is that I make my own rules—or set my own limit."

Gideon had seldom been so deeply satisfied. Here was a man

seeking the kind of integrity which he had always sought, finding it was almost impossible, and that he had to break his own and the general rules. But he did so without making excuses, without lying to himself.

"I wish everyone here had the same objective approach," Gideon sid. "There's a never-ending problem of deciding when to stretch the rules and when not to."

"I hoped you felt that way."

"Day in, day out," said Gideon, heavily. He stood up, slowly. "We must have a chat about it soon, when we aren't under pressure. Would you and your wife care to come round one Sunday, for lunch?"

As soon as he started the invitation, he realized that it was the wrong thing, sensed the barrier being erected at the very moment when he seemed so much closer to Hobbs. He should have been patient a little longer. But the question had been put, and he could not pretend to ignore the fact that Hobbs didn't answer.

Hobbs said, with great care: "Thank you. It won't be possible." There was another long pause, and in it Gideon no longer felt annoyed with himself, but began to sense that it had been the right thing to do. "My wife isn't able to get about much. She suffers from Landry's paralysis. She isn't really mobile and isn't likely to get much better, but the doctors keep the paralysis in check."

And I didn't *know*, thought Gideon. For a moment he almost hated himself. He sensed the pain which this quiet man felt, had an impression of deep emotion nearer the surface than he had ever seen it. He did not know what to say, but had to speak.

He said, slowly, effortfully: "My wife and I lost our last child. The fact that it was the seventh didn't make any difference. Ever since, I've been trying to find out why it had to happen."

Hobbs said: "Yes. Why? The never-ending question." After a pause, he gave a quick, bright smile. "I suppose we ought to get back to the Transport problem."

"That's what we're paid for," Gideon agreed. The mood changed. "You know, I think there's a way in which we might satisfy Corrington—or pacify him, if that's the better word—and keep the door open for negotiations. We don't want labour trouble on the buses and tube any more than he does. Boman says there hasn't been a lot of petty thieving going on, but that it's been increasing lately." Gideon placed his hand heavily on the file. "Seventeen depots have reported thefts from cloakrooms and rest rooms in the past six months. None of it's serious, but only three people have been caught—a coloured cleaner, a male clerk from the depot manager's office, and an elderly train driver. The cleaner was given a warning, the other two prosecuted. The clerk got six months, the tube driver was bound over. He lost his pension—that was punishment enough, the court said. So there are fourteen depots where there have been thefts by unknown people—and there's no reason why Boman shouldn't make a formal request to the yard for help on it. He could build the situation up. The Press will give him a good show, and the door will be open for our chaps, who can keep a look-out in other directions."

Hobb's eyes were narrowed and his lips curving in that rather wry smile.

"Very clever," he commented. "Shall I look after it?"

"Yes. Put it to Corrington himself, if you have a chance."

"He'll see me," said Hobbs. "In fact he's waiting to see me." He stood up and chuckled. "And all done without even bending the rules and regulations."

Unexpectedly, he held out his hand.

"Yes," said Corrington, an hour later. "I think that's an excellent proposal. Will you arrange it?"

"At once," promised Hobbs.

About that time, Ivy Kenworthy was standing at the gas

stove in her mother's kitchen. It was a small terrace house in Whitechapel, one of those which had been untouched during the bombing, and not yet on the schedule for demolition under slum clearance. The three rooms on the top floor were let to a young married couple with two babies, one of them only a month old, and with Ivy's own two children down here, it was overcrowded. The children being out at school was a help, but as she sprinkled salt into the water before putting potatoes on, she thought of the café, and how much she had enjoyed the work there. Tears stung her eyes when she remembered what had happened only two days ago. The mood of furious anger had lasted for twenty-four hours. She could still work herself up into a rage, but it did not last so long, and dismay and unhappiness crept up on her much more often today.

What had Jack done?"

Why had he been compelled to obey Bert Symes?

Remember, Symes had been a close friend of Arty Gill. She knew about Arty's death. She also knew that he was suspected of a murder. She remembered how often he had come to the café, how often he and Jack had sat at the same table, doing some business or other. "He's my unofficial bookie," Jack had told her, and she had always believed that. Could she believe it any longer?

There was a tap at the front door, not loud, but sounding clearly along the narrow passage. She dusted the salt off her hands into the water, wiped her hands on her apron, and took it off; at home she was always fastidious in her habits. She hurried along, half hoping that this was Jack.

It was Symes.

The longer she stood looking at him, the more the expression in his dark eyes scared her.

"What do you want?" she demanded, tense with apprehension.

"I want a little talk," he said, and moved forward.

She did not move aside at first. He came very close to her, without raising his arms, without clenching his hands. She wanted to refuse to allow him to enter, but as his body touched hers, as if he would simply thrust her backwards by his physical strength, her nerve broke, and she backed away. He followed her into the little front room, where the children's beds were already made. She stood with her back to the window, looking at his swarthy face, feeling more and more frightened.

"Love your kids?" he demanded suddenly.

"Of course I do!"

"Sure."

"What—what are you talking about?"

"Just making sure you love your kids," he said. "If the police come and ask you questions, you keep quiet. Understand? Your loving husband will keep quiet—seen him lately?"

"I—no." She was gasping for breath now, her breast rising and falling. "No, he—he's not been here."

"You go back to him," Symes ordered. "Take the kids and go back—he needs someone to help mend his face." Very deliberately Symes raised his right hand, and she saw the brass spikes on a band round his fingers. "And don't say a word to the police if they ask you any questions. If you do—you won't have any kids to love any longer. Understand?"

Ivy felt icy cold.

"I asked you a question," he said, and he moved his right arm, took her wrist, and began to twist. His grip was extremely painful, and pain streaked right up as far as her elbow. "I asked you if you understand."

"Yes. Yes, I do! Let me go."

"Just remember what I've told you," Symes said. "Go back to Jack tonight, as soon as the kids are home from school, and keep mum."

He let her go, stared intensely for a few seconds, then turned on his heel and went out. He slammed the door. She stood quite still, rubbing her wrist slowly; it still hurt, especially where he had gripped her, but the pain up the arm had gone.

She had never been really frightened before.

Detective Sergeant Percival King, of the NE Division, had no idea that Mrs. Kenworthy had received a visitor earlier. He approached the little house just before one o'clock, knowing exactly what he wanted to do. The Boss, Christie, had briefed him in person. He was to find out how well her husband had known Gill, and he was to find out if they knew where Gill had got his money from. King was a middle-aged man, disappointed but not yet soured because he had not reached an inspector's rank; in fact he was still determined to. Every case he worked on might be his great chance.

It was a long time before a door opened, and he heard a woman's footsteps—approaching as if hesitantly. He did not knock again. He heard the moment the lock was turned, and watched the door open. He had a queer feeling—that some kind of danger lurked behind the door.

Instead, it was Mrs. Kenworthy.

She was quite a looker in her rather big-boned way, a blonde with a Scandinavian appearance about her. Her big, fine grey eyes had a hurt look, and that didn't really surprise him, because everything he had been told suggested that she was fond of her Jack.

"Good morning," he said, brightly. "Mrs. Kenworthy?"

"Yes." She was frowning, and King got the impression that she had a very heavy load on her mind.

"I wonder if you can spare me a few minutes," King went on. "I'm Detective Sergeant King, of—" he didn't finish, but took a card out of his pocket.

He nearly missed the change in her expression when glancing down to get the card, but just managed to catch it. He knew it too well: fear. The kind of fright which leapt into the eyes of people with guilty consciences, who had not expected to be questioned.

"I can't see you now," she said, hurriedly. "My mother's ill, I can't spare—"

"Did you know Arty Gill, Mrs. Kenworthy?"

"I—I tell you I haven't any time!" This was much more than nervousness, much more than unhappiness because of a quarrel with her husband.

"Now don't be silly," King said sharply. "Don't want me to have to take you round to the station, do you? That won't help your mother. I've just seen your husband, and he's been badly knocked about. Who did it?"

"I don't know!" She was gasping. "I didn't know he'd been hurt."

"Don't be silly," repeated King. "You must have known. Who did it? What's all this about?"

"I don't know anything," she said desperately. "I can't help it if you take me to the station, I've done nothing wrong. I don't know a thing, not a thing."

She's lying, King told himself with growing excitement, and he tried to decide quickly the best way to handle her. He did not realize that such indecision was the real cause of his lack of promotion. He knew some aspects of crime very well indeed, and few men were more adept in dealing with old lags and habitual criminals, but he did not know how to deal with people who slipped up only occasionally—and the law-abiding population who found themselves involved in crime almost by accident. Twice he had taken suspects along to the station for questioning without real justification; he would never know to what trouble Christie had gone to avoid an arrest suit.

Now, big and domineering, he looked down at this woman. He read her fear—and unexpectedly, he felt sorry for her. But he spoke to her roughly.

"You know plenty," he said. "If you've got any sense, you'll tell us what's going on. You think about it. I'll be back this afternoon. I want to know all you can tell me about Arty Gill, and what he did when he was at your café. And I want to know why you walked out on your husband, too. Don't get anything wrong, Mrs. Kenworthy—you'll be in trouble if you don't tell the truth."

He turned on his heel, and walked away.

Further along the street, a youth watched until the door closed, and then jumped on to a motor scooter and raced round to Chris's garage to report to Bert Symes.

That afternoon, Gideon sat staring at an interrogation mark inside a circle, with the name *Arty G.* pencilled above it. Something had been on the tip of his tongue that morning, and he still couldn't place it. Lemaitre was talking quietly into a telephone. *Arty G—?* What was it all about?

Quite suddenly, Gideon remembered.

If the obvious was true, Arty Gill had killed the man Dean on the bus, and so indirectly caused the death of Dean's wife. Then he had gone to Winifred Wylie's one room, and killed her. Yet no one had seen a white man going along the street, and Gideon was quite sure that a white man must have been noticeable—as Hobbs had once pointed out. The killer of the bus conductress might have been coloured—*or someone who could easily pass for coloured.* He must tell Christie to look out for any friend or associate of Arty Gill who could get by as a Jamaican.

He picked up a receiver, and was soon talking to Christie.

"Just in time, George," Christie said. "I'm sending two of our chaps round to talk to this Mrs. Kenworthy—you remember I told you about her. One of my sergeants says that she's so scared she could burst into hysterics. He gave her a few hours to think things over. There isn't any doubt that she knew Gill, he was often at her café—I'll tell my man to work on this coloured angle. Thanks, George."

15

Causes of Fear

IVY KENWORTHY sat on one of the small chairs in the front room, looking at the beds where her children would sleep tonight—or where they *should* sleep. She could not get the picture of Symes's face out of her mind. She felt quite sure that he would carry out his threat, that her children were in danger.

There were other causes for fear.

Jack had been badly bashed; the police wouldn't have said so if that wasn't true, and Symes had confirmed it. She could picture Symes, with his right hand raised and the brass knuckleduster over the fingers—a weapon which could lacerate a man's face, which *had* lacerated Jack's. It was awful. She ought to be with Jack, but—*why* had he been beaten up?

Symes had come to frighten her into silence about the association between Jack and Arty Gill, she realized, and had probably beaten up Jack for that same reason. She knew her husband only too well. She knew about his big ideas, and had long suspected that he was on the fringe of crime, but it had not greatly troubled her. Now, she hated it and all it meant, because it looked as if some great slimy hand was stretching out to threaten her children.

She was frightened for them even more than for her husband.

What was the best thing to do? Should she stay here until that policeman came again? Or should she just run away—go back home, perhaps, and see Jack, and talk to him? Should she go to the school and collect the children? They would be all right in school, but what would happen to them on the way home?

There was an hour yet. She had time to go and see Jack, she had time to talk to the policeman, she had time to sit in her dread, and try to make up her mind what she ought to do.

Hildegard Delancy knew that he was being followed, but did not know by whom.

It was the middle of the afternoon. He had been at home all day, fussed over by his mother. He had not told her much, had not told her anything of the fear which seemed to eat into his body—fear that someone really was trying to kill him. All she knew was that he had been out with "some girl" and been knocked down by a car.

It *couldn't* be coincidence, could it?

First the tube station, then the car. No, it couldn't be coincidence, someone meant to kill him.

But—*why?*

The question was like a cry of anguish in his mind. *Why, why, why?* What had he done to make anyone want him dead?

Why had it happened now, when he was desperately in love, when life had taken on a whole new meaning? His fear even blotted out the face of Emily Smith, even smeared the memories of their brief love, their ever deepening love.

He couldn't *be* absolutely positive, but he felt sure that two men were following him, and he did not know either of them. One was on foot, one was on a cycle. He had seen them in Littleton Street, where he lived, when he had left to take this walk. He wished that it was half past five instead of half past three; then he would be able to go to Ealing, and see Emily. He *had* to see her soon. She had not been told what had happened yet. She would be alarmed when she did find out, and he was anxious to tell her himself.

He walked back to Littleton Street, and saw a car standing outside his home. It was a fairly big, black one, with a much longer radio aerial than most. In fact, it looked rather like a police car, but the word POLICE wasn't on it. He quickened his pace. Fears of the men behind him lessened; they could not be planning to injure him, or they would have acted by now.

Were they police?

He reached the house, a small one with a patch of garden in front, and he saw two men and a girl in the front room—two men and *Emily*. Great Scott! He thrust open the door and rushed towards the front door, but it opened before he reached it, and his mother stood there.

She was short, rather frail, rather delicate, intelligent. There was something in her expression which he didn't understand, but—*Emily*. What on earth was she doing here?

His mother held out her hands, and Delancy made himself take them, although he wanted to storm into the front room.

"What's happening? Why is Emily—?" he broke off.

"Now, now, everything's all right, dear," his mother said. "The police wanted to ask this young lady a few questions, and they want to ask you some, too. You should have told me about the Piccadilly tube accident, you know—I would have understood so much more." She drew him forward. "I think she's very nice, Gard. I do, really."

"Nice," he protested. "I—"

"Go and see her," ordered his mother.

There were two men whom he had never seen before, one looking rather like a parson, the other a bigger man. Emily was standing by the side of a chair, and when he rushed in her arms opened. For a moment he stood hugging her, oblivious of the men, even of his mother.

He did not see that his mother stood behind him, with her eyes closed as if to shut out a sight which she could not bear.

The man who looked rather like a preacher began to ask

questions. Had Delancy ever noticed that he had been followed before the attack at the tube station? Could he describe the man who had pushed him? Had he seen the driver of the car? Had he seen anyone who looked like the man who had pushed him, anywhere except at the station?

And, quite firmly:

"Do you know of any reason why anyone should want to see you dead, Mr. Delancy?"

Emily cried: "It's wicked." She jumped to her feet. "You're the police, why don't you make sure that nothing can happen to him? Why don't you?"

Bowls player Corbett of LI listened to the report of this inquiry, and talked earnestly to Parsons. It now seemed certain that Chindini's were involved, although neither man could imagine how.

"Looks to me as if Gee-Gee ought to have a go at this himself," Corbett suggested.

"I fancy he's going to," said Parsons. "I gave him a list of the directors, only this morning."

Gideon was in fact studying the list, and trying to make up his mind about what action to take.

That same afternoon, Bert Symes though outwardly composed was inwardly on edge and fearful, realizing that a net was closing round him, wondering if he could escape it. At that moment he was debating whether to snatch the Kenworthy kids or not. It would be easy enough, providing that bloody woman hadn't squealed.

But of course she wouldn't squeal, any more than Kenworthy would! They were too terrified.

He would *have* to take those kids. He wouldn't harm them. That was one of his few defensive thoughts. He needn't harm them. He could get hold of a car, pinch one, and tell the kids he was going to take them to their Dad. They'd fall for that. It would be easy.

The problem was, where to take them?

He had to have them somewhere safe, where they wouldn't be found—so that he could keep up the pressure on the Kenworthys until the heat was off.

He went across to the elderly attendant in charge of the garage, told him he would be back in half an hour, slipped out of his boiler suit, and borrowed an Austin Cambridge—a car which was too common to be noticed. He still had not decided where to take the kids.

Kenworthy's wife didn't know how lucky she was; she should be Kenworthy's widow! The thought made Symes grin; and he seldom smiled or laughed, except mockingly.

As he turned the corner of the road where the fine new modern school was, he saw the little gathering of parents, and he wondered suddenly whether Mrs. Kenworthy would be there. He drove slowly past, studying the parents. There were twelve—ten women and two elderly men, probably grandpas. Symes was quite sure the woman he was interested in wasn't among them. He felt an easing of his fears as he turned round at the far end of the street. By that time, children were beginning to run out of the school. A white-coated crossing attendant was walking into the middle of the road, to bar the way with his stop sign, and that suited Symes. He had seen the Kenworthy kids several times, and was sure he would recognize them.

There they were!

He drove past the old man in the white coat, who was now herding a mass of children on the kerb. The two Kenworthys, aged seven and eight, were hand in hand, and skipping along, gay and oblivious.

He drew up alongside.

"Hi, you kids," he called. "Like a ride?"

They stopped and turned to look at him. The girl had long hair which hung in ringlets to her shoulders, and eyes uncannily like her mother's. The dark-haired boy was more like Kenworthy, but had his mother's clear grey eyes, too.

"Yes, please," the girl said.

"Who are you?" asked the boy as if reciting a well-learned phrase.

"Oh, you know me," he said. "I'm a friend of your father." He leaned forward and opened the door, glancing in the mirror as he did so, hoping that no one was taking any particular notice of what he was doing. The girl put a small foot on the inside of the car, and the boy gave her a push.

"Hurry up, Jill!"

"That's the boy, Jack," Symes said. He was thinking: *there's an old shed down by Middle Way Wharf. That'll be the place.* He put a hand for the girl to take, and she came and bounced beside him. The boy sprang in after her, and tried to close the heavy door. "Let me," said Symes, and stretched across.

As he did so, a big man appeared by the nearside door. When Symes started back, another appeared on his side of the car. He sat there hardly breathing.

"So you were going to use the kids," one of the men said in a hard voice. Symes knew him slightly, as Detective Sergeant King. "Open this door and get out."

Symes thought, wildly, of slamming into bottom gear and making a dash for it, but the man who was now helping the puzzled children out leaned inside and took the key out of the ignition.

"I had to tell the police, I just had to," Ivy said in a hoarse voice. "He would have kidnapped the children—he would, Jack. Why, he tried to! He actually tried to. If I hadn't told the police, God knows what would have happened. Jack, say something—I tell you I had to tell the police."

Kenworthy moistened his lips.

"You had to tell them," he said in a croaky voice. "It's okay, Ivy. I'm not sore." He looked at her, and she hated the sight of his bruised and lacerated face, patched here and there with adhesive plaster and with lint; it looked as if it hurt him even to move his lips. "I—I'm just . . . I don't know what they'll do to *me*. If—if it's a murder charge—"

"But it won't be. *You* didn't know anything about it. Jack, don't be frightened. The worst is over. It is, really—all but the waiting. I'll wait for you as long as necessary. I'll have the children to look after, and the café—I'll wait for you."

Something like wonder showed in Kenworthy's dark eyes; then tears came. But fear was greater.

"And Symes only had to blacken his face a bit to pass for a Jamaican anywhere," Christie told Gideon. "It'll take a day or two to get the evidence, but we'll get him for murder all right. I've encouraged Kenworthy to turn Queen's Evidence, told him it will help in the long run."

"If he didn't take any part in the killing or the plotting it certainly will," Gideon said.

He rang off, much more pleased with the day than he had hoped to be; few days which started off so badly ended so well. Now and again he thought of Hobbs, and Hobbs's wife; he was at once exhilarated by the discovery of Hobbs as a person and as a policeman, and depressed by the truth about his married life.

The Hobbs's didn't live very far from Hurlingham—a fairly short bus ride. It might be possible one day to get Kate to meet Mrs. Hobbs.

Gideon had a final look through all the files, and left for home about half past six. He was pondering most of the way home through traffic which was thinning, but going too fast. At least the Embankment was fairly clear of heavy vehicles and the stench of diesel smoke. He wished Ringall could make quicker progress over the Seaside Strangler; Gideon had a curiously gloomy feeling about that case. By the end of the week there ought to be some kind of picture of the bus and train depot situation, however, that was a brighter side. The last word he'd had from Parsons about the two attacks on young Hildegard Delancy hadn't promised too much progress. According to Emily Smith, the man who had pushed Delancy at Piccadilly was tall, about thirty-five, dressed in brown, and had receding hair. The thing which might eventually prove to be the most helpful, however, was a slight scar on his right nostril. Parsons said that Emily was a bright little thing; she must be, if she was so observant.

Gideon had not yet decided how to set to work on Chindinis, for the board of the company contained some very big names, and it was essential to use the right tactics. It was a large company with a lot of influence.

Delancy was almost certainly still in danger, but now that they knew, they could watch and protect him. There was plenty of time to decide how best to tackle the manufacturing chemists.

16

Invitation To The Seaside

"LIKE it?" asked George Cope.

"It's glorious," said Peggy Blessington, her eyes glowing.

"Like a bit more speed?"

"Ooh, yes, please!"

They were on the Great West Road, heading for London Airport, after driving along the broad highway, with its three traffic lanes in each direction, at over a hundred miles an hour already. George Cope did this in short stretches only, and kept slowing down. He was very pleased with the way things were working out. Peggy was just the girl. The thought made him laugh. *Just the girl.* It had taken him two weeks to break her in, for she had twice refused invitations for a drive in his Jaguar. When at last she had fallen for the invitation, she had been a little nervous.

That didn't worry him at all.

She hadn't really believed that he had a Jaguar, of course. But he had one of the low-flying, frog-like sports models which swept along the road as if it were about to take off. It was black and shiny, and all the lamps at the front made it look like a creature with a dozen blind eyes. Once Peggy had realized that he hadn't been boasting, she had been much more relaxed. And then he had discovered that she was one of those girls who loved speed.

A lot of girls were nervous, even though they professed to like it; it was easy to tell, from the way they held on to the seat or the door handles. Peggy Blessington had no thought of fear. She sat back, eyes narrowed, lips parted, body relaxed—and when she was dressed in a light cotton frock, as she was now, what a body!

Cope put his foot down. All the other traffic seemed to stand still. Then he had to jam on his brakes for a red traffic light, just beyond a thirty mile limit sign, and jolted to a standstill. Peggy laughed.

"Like it?" Cope demanded again.

"It's wonderful!"

"Only one trouble."

"What's that, George?"

"As soon as we've started, we have to stop."

"Yes, I know."

"Peg—" he began, and broke off, as if diffidently.

"Yes?"

"Would you think I'd got a nerve if—"

The lights changed. He broke off, deliberately, and roared off, leaving an M.G. and a Vauxhall standing. A little further ahead was a grey Bentley. Cope brayed on his horn, the Bentley changed lanes, the Jaguar raced past it as the Bentley driver gave him a scathing look. Cope laughed. By then they were close to the end of the three lane highway, and it was not until they had turned off the next road opposite London Airport, that he stopped and pulled into the side road. He handled the car beautifully, and soon they were facing the airport. A jet came screaming in, and as they watched it, landing lights aglow, Cope saw that the girl's eyes were still very bright; anything to do with speed obviously fascinated her.

He slid his arm round her shoulders and rested it there lightly. The roaring of engines faded for a few minutes.

She turned to look at him.

"George."
"Yes, old girl?"
"What were you going to say?"
"Was I going to say something?"
"You know you were."
"You're thinking of some other chap."
"I'm not." She sat up, indignantly. "I don't usually let men ake me around in their expensive sports cars."
"That's good."
He began to stroke her neck with his forefinger.
"George, what *were* you going to say?"
"I don't remember—oh, yes. About the short spells in the ar. Fast spells, I mean."
"That's right."
"Well, I was going to say that if we could get out on to one of he trunk roads, the MI maybe, it would be easy to open her ight out. Or the Brighton Road has fast patches. Nothing like he MI, though. I was going to ask—oh, forget it."
"I don't want to forget it!"
"Now you're shouting at me," he teased. He kept stroking her neck with his forefinger, quite lightly. "I was going to ask if you could get off for the week-end. There are some wonderful places we could spend a week-end, by the sea, or—Do you know Stratford-on-Avon?"
"I've seen pictures of it."
"*Pictures!*"
"I'm just a simple working girl, you know."
"Not so simple," said Cope, half seriously. "You ought not to be wasting your time as a messenger—you ought to be a model, or something like that. It would suit you much better."
"*Thank* you, kind sir."
"No, I mean it."
"So do I!"
"Peg, how about the week-end?" asked Cope, suddenly earnest. He moved his arm, twisted round, took her hands and sat so that they faced each other. Dusk was upon them, and the

afterglow shone on her face and in her eyes, giving them a limpid look. Her complexion seemed dreamlike, and so did the full curve at her breast. He knew better than to try any familiar stuff tonight, though; she had to leave him thinking that he was the world's most well-behaved gentleman. "There's a little place on the river, near Henley-in-Arden. Absolutely lovely spot. We could do a bit of boating as a change from speed—and we could have two or three runs on the M1—do you know I did thirty miles in fifteen minutes on it, a few weeks ago."

"You didn't."

"I certainly did. What about it, Peg? It's a nice little country pub, never more than half a dozen people staying there, although they do a good bar trade, and the food's just right."

"It sounds wonderful," she said, wistfully.

"It would be wonderful, if only you'd come."

"Let me think about it," Peggy procrastinated.

"All right," Cope agreed. A note of disappointment sounded in his voice—one which he did not really feel. He was quite sure that the answer would soon be yes—if not this week-end, then next. He sat there screwing up some old bus tickets which had collected in his pocket, got out and put them in a litter-basket fastened to a tree. Peggy watched every movement he made. He got back, and rested his right arm on her shoulder, and began to stroke the curve with his forefinger again. Her skin was so lovely and smooth—lovely and smooth—lovely and smooth. He liked girls with lovely smooth necks. He *loved* them. He loved lying with them, after winning them over, and liked to smooth them and caress them, and then feel their necks beneath his fingers, and then to exert a gentle pressure which they seldom minded, because he had done it before, and finally to squeeze and squeeze—

It was the most exhilarating experience in the world.

The problem about the week-end, for Peggy Blessington, was really a commonplace one. Her parents certainly would not approve of her going off for a week-end on her own, although they might agree if she was supposed to be going in a foursome. George certainly wouldn't want that, and she didn't, either; another couple would spoil things. But if it were the only means of getting away together, they would have to accept it.

She could trust George absolutely; she felt quite sure of that. She had a sense of rightness whenever she was with him; even the touch of his fingers gave her a feeling of security.

Then it seemed as if the fates were conspiring to prove how "right" her love was, for when she got home from her messenger-rounds a day or two later, she found her parents excited because they had been invited to spend a long week-end with some relations in Cornwall, in three weeks time. They had only one anxiety; leaving Peggy here on her own.

"Oh, I'll be all right, Mum. As a matter of fact," went on Peggy brightly, "some of the girls at the office are making up a party for a week-end up at Stratford-on-Avon. You know, Shakespeare's place. I think it's the very week-end you're going. I might as well go, mightn't I?"

"Very good idea," her father approved. "It's better than being here on your own—and you'll be improving your mind at the same time."

All of them laughed. Peggy hoped that she did not sound or seem as happy as she felt.

"I hate waiting so long," George Cope grumbled, the next morning. They were on a Number 15 bus together—he often joined her on her rounds, now. "But if that's the earliest we can make it—roll on September 27th!"

Paddy O'Neil did not hear what he said, but he noticed how closely they sat together. He knew it was absurd but he felt something akin to jealousy, and his cheerful "fares plaize" was subdued for twenty minutes or so.

Then a plump colleen from Connemara got on, and he cheered up the moment he heard her soft brogue.

* * *

On Thursday morning, Gideon heard a noise near him as he gradually woke from a heavy sleep, and opened one eye. The noise, a rumbling, stopped. He could not see, the lashes were gummed together, and vision was blurred. He had a momentary thought that a blind man must feel something like this. Then he opened both eyes wide, realizing that Kate was standing by his side, half laughing.

He was on his back.

"It's a miracle you don't wake yourself," Kate said.

He echoed: "Wake myself?" Then he added unwisely: "What with?"

Kate laughed.

"Oh, not that again," said Gideon, suddenly comprehending. "If a man can't give a gentle snore—"

He stopped, remembering the noise that had woken him, and suspecting that he had in fact woken himself. He felt the half irritated, half ashamed feeling that he usually did, especially if he had disturbed Kate, and it looked as if he had this morning. He sat up. Kate wore a lightweight dressing-gown with a lily pattern on it—a family birthday present last year. Her greying hair was brushed, and she had on a touch of lipstick, but no rouge. She looked bright-eyed and very well.

"What time is it?" Gideon asked.

"Just turned eight."

"Did I wake you?"

"Not this morning. I woke myself, and you were almost quiet. I thought I'd find out what it was like to get up early again, and make the tea. It feels wonderful!" She sat on the foot of the bed, leaning forward and began to pour out. "I think your breakfast time labours are over. I feel so much better."

"Now don't you start overdoing it," Gideon protested. But it was good to sit up and drink tea and to know that he could take his time shaving and bathing. He could not think of much likely to worry him at the office this morning—in fact he had cancelled a briefing spell, leaving it to Lemaitre today, so that he could talk with Parsons, Hobbs and Boman about the results of the first two weeks' work at the bus depots. So far, nothing really sensational had developed, although there was rather more petty stealing than Boman had reported. Thinking of Hobbs set Gideon thinking about his paralysed wife. He hadn't told Kate about her, yet—He did so.

"From what you say you'll have to do it tactfully, but of course I'd like to go and see her," Kate said. "I'm not sure it wouldn't do her good to come out here, if she can get into a wheel chair. See what you can find out, dear."

"I will," promised Gideon.

He was in a bright mood when he reached the office, and it was only slightly dimmed when Lemaitre glanced across, adjusted his tie, and reported:

"Got a real treat for you this morning, George. Whiskey galore—all from Ould Oireland. Llandudno police think that a lot of the real stuff is being smuggled in, and a lot is being sold at ten bob off the wholesale price in some of the outlying districts—sold to pubs, I mean. They think it would be a good idea if we could send up someone who isn't Welsh or Irish, preferably one who looks like a Londoner on holiday. Couldn't spare me for a few days, could you?"

"I can always spare you," said Gideon, "but I've got somewhere else for you to go. Underground." He grinned. "What next?"

"Ringall would like a word, before he goes off to Bournemouth again."

"He found something?"

"He sounded as if he'd lost a pound and found a sixpence."

"Hmm," grunted Gideon. "Oh, well. Get him in."

He had a distinct impression that Ringall was getting fatter, especially at the jowl and neck. He filled the office door and overlapped the chair in front of the desk. His heavy-lidded eyes had no brightness at all, and he was breathing stertorously. Gideon thought: he needs a rest.

"Morning, Ring. Had any luck?"

"Luck? I'd forgotten there was any such thing," complained

Ringall. "We got that fingerprint on the locket, and we got the fingerprint on the envelope and the two bus tickets, but that's about it. I've personally questioned the car park attendants—all they do is laugh, they have their work cut out to make sure no one gets in without paying his fee in the summer—the parks are crowded out. I've quesitoned every conductor on the Number 15 route, too. I've shown 'em photographs of the dead girls—got two to say they *thought* they'd seen one of the girls, but that's about it. Absolute blank ever since."

"Pity," said Gideon.

"George—you know I'm no slacker, don't you?"

"Slacker?" Gideon was surprised. Then his spirits rose, because this seemed to presage exactly the right thing. "I should say you put more man hours into the job than anyone else we've got."

"Except you, George," said Ringall. "Always except you. The truth is, I think I'm overtired. I worry about this job too much. Hardly slept for the last three nights, it's on my mind so much. I think I'd be wise to have a break—get on to some other job, George. Think you can fix it?"

Ringall's breathing was even more laboured.

"You know what, don't you," said Gideon. "You ought to take a couple of weeks' leave."

"That's what my wife says, but—well, I'm not sure I would be happy hanging about and doing nothing. I've got a feeling that if I could just keep going, but not have the girls on my mind so much, it would be a help."

Ringall was running his fingers over his mouth, and Gideon was smoothing the bowl of his pipe.

"I'll tell you what we have got," Gideon said. "Came in this morning. Llandudno's a bit bothered over smuggling from Ireland—whiskey, mostly. They asked if we could spare a man. How about going up there and taking your wife with you?"

When a delighted Ringall had gone, fully briefed, and with spritely step, Gideon pondered for a few minutes before seeing Parsons, Hobbs and Boman. They arrived together, and

Gideon watched closely to judge how well they were integrated. He did not think that Parsons or Boman was in the slightest degree self-conscious with Hobbs. They had been working together long enough to know the job inside out, and had come firmly to the conclusion that there was no connection between the attacks on Delancy and the robberies. They had come even more firmly to the conclusion that Chindini's must be involved in the attacks on Delancy, and the deaths of the other three people in front of tube trains.

Gideon made a decision there and then, one which he knew must have been hovering in his subconscious for a long time.

"I'll go and see Chindini's Managing Director myself. He might be able to give us a lead. This is a case for coming right out with it, not for sneaking about. How about the thefts from the depots and bus stations, Beau?"

Boman pursed his lips, and looked uncomfortable. Hobbs took out cigarettes, and offered them. Boman looked at the packet, selected a cigarette, said "Ta" and then started to speak very quickly.

"None so blind as those who won't see, George. As a matter of fact, I've had a bit of a shock. Couldn't see the wood for the trees, but—well, the last people I'd ever expect are behind the thefts. We had a tip off to look at the Museum that's run by a couple of old timers. They've spent their lives with London Transport. It's heart breaking. Funny thing, but that sergeant from NE, Percy King, the chap who made Mrs. Kenworthy talk, he checked up and found . . ."

Detective Sergeant Percival King had been very pleased with himself after the capture of Bert Symes, and the seal had been set on his pleasure when Hugh Christie had promised to recommend him for promotion. He felt on the crest of a wave. The assignment to help check the bus terminals, stations and depots in his area, and some of the Underground stations, too, came as a kind of anti-climax. He was eager to get it done. He knew the London Transport Police officers who usually worked this district, and considered himself a cut above them; no one could convince *him* that the British Transport Commission Force was on a par with the Metropolitan Police, whatever the rule book said. He did not see it—as he should have—as a distinct group, like the City of London Police, or one of the County Police organizations. He regarded it as a group of amateurs who did their own job passably well.

He was, however, fully aware that if he talked like this he would soon be on the carpet. That precious promotion might even be jeopardized, and he was determined to be on his best behaviour. He went to the Aldgate terminal; had a long talk with a police inspector in charge, and studied all the reports of thefts from the area, as well as those from neighbouring areas. His reaction was one almost of scorn; he wanted to ask how it was so many petty thefts were committed with so few arrests made, but wisely he didn't.

"If you ask me, I believe some of the cleaners or temporary hands are responsible," the local man said.

"You're probably right," said King, heartily. "Only little problem, though—it's pretty steady, isn't it? Let's have a look." He studied a chart which showed the depots from which thefts had taken place. "Spread pretty even everywhere," he remarked, and Gideon would have approved of this reasoning. "Wouldn't expect part-timers and cleaners out at Hampstead, say, or Richmond, to be as light-fingered as those around here, would you? There's a bigger crime ratio in my manor than there is in Blackheath, for instance."

"That's right," agreed the local man. "That's what Boman says."

"Does he? Looks to me as if it could be someone who goes the rounds of the various depots pretty regularly," went on King. He sat back with his hands behind his head, and squinted up. "Now, who'd that be? Special service maintenance chaps, for one. Line-Inspectors. Depot Inspectors. Bus Route Inspectors . . ."

"It's going to be a hell of a job sorting that lot out," said the local man. "But—" He broke off, moistened his lips, and went on: "I had a phone call this morning—a tip-off, it was supposed to be. Some anonymous swine said that two chaps who run the *Bus & Tube Museum* ought to be checked up on."

Before he could go on, the door opened.

The inspector sprang to his feet, for Superintendent Boman came in.

King also stood up.

King had an air of great confidence, but Boman was obviously preoccupied and worried. They could not know that he had the tube murders on his mind, and the pressure of Corrington all the time. He knew King casually, nodded, and sat down.

"Anything you'd like, Super?" asked the local man.

"I'd like to catch this so-and-so," said Boman.

"You think that it's one man, then," King put in smartly.

"One man, a couple or a group of them," said Boman. "What's on your mind?"

After a pause, the bus inspector said: "I had a tip-off this morning—someone suggested looking at Joe Ware and Fred Dibben."

King leaned forward, poking his forefinger towards Boman's chest.

"If you ask me, Mr. Boman, these thefts *are* by someone who is *trusted.* Someone who wouldn't be suspected at all. Someone who can slip in and out of the depots whenever they like. Someone—" He broke off, and a curious glitter made his eyes look like glass. "So that pair out at the *Bus & Tube Museum* look right. They can go anywhere they like, can't they? That museum must cost a lot. Eh? How about it?"

Boman was thinking sickeningly, that he had never given Joe Ware and Fred Dibben a second thought; that he had trusted them absolutely, regarding them almost as members of his own Force. He was silent for a long time, and it was the local inspector who said miserably:

"Joe and Fred? It can't be."

"We'd better take a look, and ask a few questions," said King, airily. "Like me to look around? It would be better for me—easier, I mean. If you're a pal of these chaps—" He broke off, making his implication clear enough by his silence. "I could take a couple of men along and make a routine search. Shall I do that?"

Boman said: "It *can't* be them." But he was apprehensive, because vaguely he understood the possible consequences if such a suspicion were justified. The shadow of Corrington seemed to be looming over his shoulder: Corrington telling him to leave this to the Yard men, to give the Yard men plenty of scope. "I don't think you'll find anything, but you'd better have a look," he said grudgingly. "Take it easy with those two."

"They won't be there this morning, they're both on duty," interpolated the Aldgate Inspector. "I happen to know old Charley Lime is standing in for Joe Ware, and Lucy Dibben's doing the Underground tours this morning. Charley lives next door to me, that's how I know."

"Just the time for a search," said King cheerfully. "Don't worry, Mr. Boman—I'll handle it tactfully."

Lucy Dibben, sixty-three years old, with the figure of a woman of thirty-three, grey-haired, soft-voiced, a gentle person who always softened her husband's brittle hardness, cheerfully allowed the two Scotland Yard men to look round. King told her that two suspects had managed to hide somewhere in the area, and while Mrs. Dibbens did not think there was any chance of them hiding in the museum or nearby, she said that the police were quite free to look.

Half an hour later, she stared down at a collection of wallets, handbags, watches, rings, a conglomeration of small stolen goods, which had been locked in one of the big spare-parts boxes for the museum. By then, she was frightened. Of course she had never seen them before. Never. Yes, both Joe and Fred had a key to this box, they often went to it. But—*they* hadn't put these things there. These—were these *stolen* goods?

Mrs. Ware, Isabel to her close friends, was a stout, plump, merry woman, who had borne seven children—all of whom came home every Christmas, so happy was her family. When Lucy Dibben arrived, "Looking like death warmed up, she was really," she immediately thought: *There's been an accident.* When Lucy told her what had happened, she was horrified, stunned—and frightened.

Mrs. Dibben knew that the police were going to be at the Museum, ready for Joe and Fred, and both women hurried there.

Dibben and Ware, travelling on the same bus, got off at the Museum without even a thought of trouble. The first intimation was the sight of Boman—and the expression on his face. Then, in the entrance hall which had been cleared of visitors, the two wives waited in obvious dread.

"Hey! What's going on?" demanded Dibben.

Ware looked startled . . .

It was King, cocky and inwardly elated, who told them, while Boman stood by.

Dibben's deep-set eyes were burning, his hands were clenched, he looked as if he would like to throw himself at Boman. Joe Ware had a baffled expression as he leaned against one of the old buses, where the goods had been found. His eyes were half closed, as if in defeat.

"If you think I'd have anything to do with this racket you're a fool," Dibben said. "I thought you were a friend."

"Listen, Fred, we found the stuff here. If you can tell us how it got here—"

"Well, I can't. *I* didn't put it there, and nor did Joe."

"Joe—" Boman began, and he moistened his lips, hating all this—and disliking Detective Sergeant King, who stood by as if he were gloating. "Joe, what can you tell me?"

"Nothing at all," replied Joe Ware. He opened his eyes very

wide. "I've never seen them before. You ought to know that. I didn't think you would ever bring in officers from Scotland Yard to spy on us."

King did not correct him, by substituting "Division" for "Scotland yard."

"Listen, you two," Boman said desperately. "If you can't explain how this stuff came to be here I'll have to put you both on a charge. I can't help myself. God knows I don't want to, but that's evidence. Don't you understand?"

"I've never seen any of it before," said Dibben harshly.

"Never in my life." Ware seemed to sigh.

"I think we ought to take them round to the station for questioning," King said. He straightened up, decisively, and Boman knew that he was right.

There were tears in Mrs. Dibben's eyes, and fear in Mrs. Ware's.

"And when they got them to the Division and searched them, Ware had a copule of cigarette lighters in his pocket—two lighters were reported lost this morning—and Dibben had more money than you'd expect, and a watch which belonged to one of the bus drivers," Boman said to Gideon. "There can't be any serious doubt that they're guilty, George. The hell of it is, I took 'em both on trust. Actually asked them to help me." While Gideon didn't speak, Parsons simply looked ill-at-ease, and Hobbs stood almost at attention, Boman went on: "That museum's taken every penny of their savings. It's been their life. Every penny they've taken for admission has gone back into it, and to charities. I've known them for years. They live in the same little homes where they always have. They actually skimp themselves to make improvements for that museum. It's a real tragedy."

"Are you quite sure there isn't any doubt?" Hobbs inquired.

"I can't *see* any," Boman admitted. "God knows what Corrington is going to say!"

"Supposing we go along and see Corrington together," Hobbs suggested.

"Do that, will you?" Gideon approved.

When Hobbs and Boman went out together, Parsons exchanged glances with Gideon, and Lemaitre stood up from his desk, smoothed his hand over his thinning hair, came forward, and said:

"If he goes on like this, Hobbs will be almost human one day. Sounded proper sorry for Beau, didn't he?"

"Who doesn't?" asked Gideon. "Vic, get the most detailed reports possible, will you? Go over and talk to Christie, see this chap King, and then see the two wives. I've got a feeling that there are going to be a lot of repercussions over this."

"How do you mean?" Parsons was almost sharp-voiced.

"Don't be daft," said Lemaitre. "He's just got a feeling."

At that very moment, word was being spread around six bus depots and two railway workshops, that Joe and Fred had been arrested for theft, and that the Board had called in Scotland Yard—had been *spying* on the workers. Meetings were to be held that afternoon, in protest.

Higson and the Action Committees were all set to act.

Parsons finished his talk with Detective Sergeant King, and felt much as Boman had; he did not like the Divisional man, who was hard-voiced and too self-assured, but there seemed no fault in what he had done. Perhaps due to Boman's presence, he had been as helpful as he could with Ware and Dibben. Both men were now at Divisional Headquarters. Each had been allowed to say goodbye to his wife, at home, and to take some comforts to the cells.

Christie had seen them when they had arrived.

"Dibben was breathing fire, but Ware looked as if he would collapse at any minute," Christie said. He was at attention, as he always seemed to be when under any kind of pressure. "I had a doctor look him over, He's all right, physically, as far as we can tell. What does Gee-Gee say?"

"Dig as deep as we can," answered Parsons. "I've got to go and see the two wives."

"Mrs. Dibben's with Mrs. Ware—and half the Ware family," Christie told him drily. "Mind they don't scratch your eyes out."

When Parsons drew up, alone, outside the small terraced house where the Wares lived, he sensed what Christie meant. Outside the front door, wheels tied to each other, were two prams. In the little porch was a scooter, a child's bow and arrow, and two cricket bats. A horde of kids were racing noisily up and down the street, but when they saw the car they swarmed about it, and a boy of about ten called out:

"He's a copper!"

"Hey, you—where's my grandpa?" another boy asked.

"He didn't steal anything, he *wouldn't,*" piped a child of six or seven.

Parsons stood with eight or nine children about him, hands together in front of his stomach, tips of the fingers touching. If the local vicar had come to give comfort he could not have parodied himself more cruelly. Yet Parsons' manner did something to quieten the children, except a boy of eleven or twelve, who said bitterly:

"Aw, cops."

"As a matter of fact, I've come to see if I can help at all," Parsons said. "I'm from the Yard, yes—" he saw how that impressed the boys, but did not wait too long before going on: "All we want to find are the guilty."

"It's not grandpa!"

"It can't be!"

He knocked at the door, and after a pause a girl in her twenties, red-faced, heavy bosomed, and with very short skirts, opened the door.

"I wonder if I can see Mrs. Ware," said Parsons, gently.

"Who wants her?"

When he told her, she looked as if she hated him, and when he was shown into the front room, he could understand why. Mrs. Ware was on the sofa, so pale that she looked near collapse. Mrs. Dibben, more in control of herself, sat by her side. Two more young women, one of them with a scarlet-faced baby in her arms, were in the room, as well as two youngish men. In a reluctant rush of introduction, Parsons gathered that these were two sons, one daughter-in-law, and two daughters.

"My Joe wouldn't do it, it's a wicked thing to say," Mrs. Ware insisted, her voice frail with shock. "It's a wicked thing to say. He's served the Transport all his life, why it's *been* his life. And to think—"

She began to cry.

"Now, Isabel, try not to upset yourself," Mrs. Dibben soothed.

"Oh, Mum." One of the daughters was nearly in tears. Another snapped at Parson: "Why did you have to come round making things worse? They were bad enough, weren't they? Who asked you to—?"

"I know just how you feel," Parsons said, still gently. "I've come with special instructions from my chief at Scotland Yard—" He paused at "Yard" again, and all of them were impressed, even Mrs. Ware. He went on quietly: "Those instructions are to try to find out if there is any possibility of a mistake. If there is—"

"It's all a mistake."

"Of course, it's a mistake."

"It's terrible, terrible," Mrs. Ware said, and closed her eyes. Tears squeezed their way through the lids.

It was going to be a terrible week-end.

It was going to be a wonderful week-end, Peggy kept telling herself; wonderful, wonderful, wonderful!

She could hardly wait.

Now and again, a whisper of doubt sounded in her head, bringing a touch of guilt, becuase she had lied to Mum and Dad, who kept talking about "improving her mind" at Stratford-on-Avon. There was another whisper of doubt, too, allied to a kind of fear. It was not of *George;* there would never be any need to fear him. It was a deeper, different, breathless fear of submitting, surrendering, giving herself to a man for the first time.

If—if only they were married.

"But we will be, soon," she told herself, and for a while stilled both her conscience and her fear.

17

Strike Call

SIR HENRY CORRINGTON sat behind his desk, without speaking, and without moving. He had heard the story, and talked a little about it, but gave much the same impression as Gideon—that he had a "feeling" of trouble. His expression showed nothing of his emotions, however, but the way his lean fingers played with a ball pen gave some indication of them. Boman, preferring to stand, was by the window. Hobbs sat on the arm of a chair.

"I assure you, Sir Henry, I had no choice at all. None at all," Boman said.

"I understand that," said Corrington. "Once we called in outside help, it was out of our hands. If I had left it to you, we could have given ourselves time to think about it. Now—" his lips twisted ruefully, he looked rather like Hobbs. "I insisted on calling in the Yard, so I can hardly blame you or the Yard for the situation, can I?"

"The devil of it is, I don't think I'd ever have got on to them!"

"Possibly not. Well—" Corrington leaned back. "I've had two reports of protest meetings, one at Hendon and one at Wimbledon. It wouldn't surprise me—"

He broke off, when a buzzer sounded in the internal communication box on his desk. He turned down a switch.

"Harry?" The voice of Colonel Tulson sounded loud and clear.

"Yes," Corrington said. "I'm with—"

"There have been two strike calls, one at Greenwich and one at Clapham," Tulson careered on. "I think there will be a walkout. They're demanding the withdrawal of the suspension of the two men until the charges have been more closely investigated. It's an impossible demand to meet, of course."

"Yes," Corrington agreed. "Quite impossible."

"The Minister would like a conference on the situation late this afternoon, to see what we can do to prevent the situation from worsening. The devil of it is—but you've got someone with you, you say."

"Boman and Hobbs."

"Oh," said Tulson. It was almost possible to see him wrinkle his nose. "All right, Henry. Six o'clock for the conference. Will that be all right?"

"Yes," said Corrington. He hesitated, then flicked off, pressed down another switch, and said to a girl who answered: "Call Lady Corrington, will you, and tell her that I don't expect to be home for dinner tonight, and that we shall have to cancel our evening engagement. Tell her I will call as quickly as I can myself." He switched off again, and gave a queer little laugh. "How apt the trite sayings are," he remarked. "Hoist with his own petard. I thought that the staff would be delighted that we'd called in help to stop this petty thieving, and that we would all get pats on the back. Instead, I've given the Action Committees the very weapon they asked for." He looked into Boman's eyes. "You say there isn't the faintest possibility that these two men are innocent?"

"They had all the stuff, actually some stolen lighters in their pockets today," Boman said. "The only vague possibility is—"

He broke off.

"Yes?"

"Well, we've checked, but there aren't any fingerprints on the stolen goods," said Boman. "If Ware and Dibben used gloves that would expalin it, but—would they use gloves *after* they'd got the stuff home? And if they've been doing this for so long, where do they sell the stuff? We're checking that. The trouble is—"

"I think I know what you mean," interrupted Corrington. "The protest meetings are bad enough, but if we found these men were innocent, we'd be in trouble for wrongful or unjustified arrest, as well as for bringing in the Yard. The Action Committees would take full advantage of it. If we hadn't called you in, Hobbs—"

Corrington broke off. It said a lot for him that he could still smile, that he shook Boman's hand firmly, and clapped him on the shoulder.

When they had gone, he telephoned his wife.

"But surely the men will see you *had* to do it," Moira Corrington said protestingly. "They can't blame you for this."

"They won't blame me, they'll blame the Board," Corrington said. "It's the Board that will blame me. Don't be too glum about it. Things may work out quite well. I've been thinking, why don't you go along to the Thorntons' dinner on your own? I'll join you if I can manage it."

"Come home as soon as you can," Moira said. "I'll be here. I never really liked General Thornton, anyhow."

Gideon sat back in the car, driven by an elderly driver through the thickening of rush our traffic. Every now and again he saw a newspaper placard reading:

BUS & TUBE
STRIKE THREAT

Now and again, when the car stopped near one of the newspaper sellers, the call came out: "*Bus Strike, Latest.*" Or else: "*More Tube Troubles.*" Another called: "*Good news for shoe shops, more walking ahead!*" Gideon smiled dourly, watching the faces of the people, knowing that Londoners could be harassed more by a transport strike than by anything. Already queues were forming at the bus stops, and as he passed Leicester Square Station on the way to Chindini's, throngs of workers were herding towards the entrances, waiting for the trains to whirl them out to the perimeter of London. Nothing could upset London's fantastically intricate organization more than such a strike.

Would it come?

He saw a placard reading: "*Two Depots out.*" He was troubled and even annoyed because that had come so quickly; it meant that somewhere a depot had been spoiling for a fight, perhaps one where the Action Committee was very strong. Would many of the workers really come out? If two trusted men had been caught virtually red-handed, how could anyone blame London Transport for instant suspension? The accused men would be in the dock tomorrow, of course.

He thought: "I wonder how Corrington will handle it. If he puts up a good London Transport Board lawyer to act for them—wonder what he's made of, really."

Then he saw the big white stone blocks of the Chindini building, and put the strike problem out of his mind. Thank God, it wasn't his to cope with.

Sir Robert Chindini had asked him to come at five-thirty, apologizing because it was so late, but that had suited Gideon's book very well.

The Chairman of Directors of Chindini Pharmaceuticals Limited was a small man with a slightly hunched back. Gideon had seen photographs of him, but never met him. He was surprised to see how like he was to the little Transport Inspector, Fred Dibben. He stood at a very large flat-topped desk, in a small office, with windows which overlooked the older part of Soho, and rounded the desk to shake hands with quick, smooth movements. Anyone seeing them must have been amused by the contrast between the small, slender man, with sharp features and very bright eyes, and the massive man with blunted features and thoughtful, almost brooding eyes.

"I'm sorry it had to be so late, Commander," Chindini said. "But I have to fly to New York tomorrow, and I shall be away for at least a week. Your message so intrigued me that I would like to hear about the problem from you. I can then delegate powers to others—but you were most emphatic that this was a confidential matter."

"Up to you who else you tell," said Gideon, and took a proffered chair. Chindini opened a corner cabinet of dark oak and took out whiskey, soda, ice, water, and two cut glasses. "It's a very tricky and awkward situation, sir. What we would like is to have one or two of our men in your headquarters here, making discreet inquiries."

"Will you have a whiskey? Or gin? Or—"

"Whiskey and soda will be just right," said Gideon. He waited until it was in his hand. "Cheers."

"Success in your endeavours," said Chindini, and smiled rather like an eagle. "You don't suspect *us* of any company fraud, I hope."

"No, this isn't a Fraud Squad job," Gideon assured him. He felt as nearly sure as he could that Chindini had no idea what he had come about, and sipped his drink and relaxed. "The truth is, sir . . ."

The story took exactly six minutes to tell, and Gideon missed no relevant point. He studied the face of the little man all the time, and he saw the thoughtful frown, the look of concentration, the look of perceptiveness on the alabaster face. When Gideon had finished he sat behind the desk with his fingers interlaced, the cut glass, reflected in the shiny wood, rather like lace-work.

"Thank you, Commander. Let me say at once that I greatly appreciate your discretion. However, I *may* be able to help quite quickly." Chindini had made no notes, but went on without a pause. "The victims of these so-called accidents were

Martha Robson, an accountant in this company; the wife of Dr. Samuel Corndelson, once of our Research Laboratory here in London; Mr. Peter Wrightson, once a laboratory assistant and more lately a pharmaceutical chemist in Clapham Common, and now another member of our accountancy staff, Hildegard Delancy. Delancy is a very able man, incidentally. I have him marked out for promotion as soon as he shows signs of accepting a greater degree of responsibility, at the moment he seems too immature." Chindini smiled. "You are surprised that I have such personal knowledge of my staff?"

"I didn't expect it."

"I'm sure that you have the same kind of knowledge of yours, and with the Divisions you have far more to cope with," Chindini declared. He spread his hands. "Commander, I may be wrong, but I think I can put you on the right track. I most certainly hope so. Some four years ago, Martha Robson held a trusted position here. She betrayed her trust, and we discovered that over several years she had defrauded the company of nearly five thousand pounds. The first hint of this came from the wife of Dr. Corndelson, who raised a query about her husband's salary and expenses. Wrightson reported, at about the same time, shortages in deliveries of certain drugs. He was worried because he thought they might have got into the wrong hands, but in fact the shortage was due to Mrs. Robson's defalcations.

"We had to have Mrs. Robson watched closely, not wanting her to be unjustly blamed or worried by questioning, unless we were sure of ourselves—we try to be human here," Chindini went on. "We put young Delancy on the job of checking her figures closely. He made an excellent job of it, and found all the defalcations. We had to accuse Mrs. Robson, and of course dismissed her. She proved to be three months pregnant at the time, and I preferred to accept her assurance that she would not try to get another job, but would settle down to domestic life. We did not prosecute. But the affair so preyed on her mind that she—ah—had an 'accident' in front of a tube train at Piccadilly. That was four months later. By then Corndelson and his wife, as well as Wrightson, had left the company—Mrs. Corndelson also to have a baby, Wrightson because he wanted to go into the retail side of the pharmaceutical business. Young Delancy was on holiday at the time. I saw no point in aggravating the situation for the bereaved husband, a verdict of Accidental Death was returned at the inquest, although I don't think there is much doubt that Mrs. Robson threw herself in front of the train."

Chindini had explained all this much as if he were lecturing to a class of students. At last he paused. His eyebrows lifted inquiringly, as if to ask:

"Do you see what I mean, Commander?"

Gideon said: "So the man Robson lost his wife and the baby."

"Ah."

"Has he ever threatened you, sir?"

"No, never."

"Did you ever give a second thought to the mysterious way these people died?"

"Commander, until you sat and told me this story I did not know the manner of their deaths. I am out of the country a great deal. No one thought it worth reporting, even if they realized who the victims were. After all, these people were no longer in my employ—all this happened nearly four years ago. Had I had the slightest indication I would have consulted Scotland Yard at once. As it is—you tell me that the man who attempted to push Delancy off the platform was rather tall, in the middle thirties, and with a slight scar on his right nostril."

"That's right," Gideon was breathing very hard. "Do you know him?"

"I saw the man Robson when he came here to collect some of his wife's belongings, immediately after she had left our employ. That happened during one of my periods in England, and I was in the Accounts Department when he came. I have a very good memory for faces, Commander. I can only tell you that this man I saw fits very closely to the description you have given me. I can give you his old address, if that will help . . ."

Emily Smith ran into her mother and father, late that evening, eyes bright and very eager.

"Mum, the police want me to go to an identification parade! They think they've found the man, I've got to see him. It'll be first thing in the morning, I've got to be there at ten o'clock. They say they'll phone the office and—Mum, do you think I could have the whole day off? Do you think it would be all right? Gard thinks *he* can get it . . ."

"What you've got to worry about is being absolutely sure," her father said.

Next morning, just after ten o'clock, ten men paraded in the courtyard at Scotland Yard, out of sight but within sound of passing traffic. They were all dressed in much the same way—brown suits, trilby hats, ties. They were all about the same age, and two of them looked remarkably alike. All but one—John Steward Robson, who had been held for questioning the night before—had been asked to come in off the Embankment or out of Parliament Street.

They stood in a line.

Parsons and a detective sergeant came out, with Emily Smith between them. She kept moistening her lips. Ever since waking she had been reminding herself that she had to be sure, absolutely sure. For it meant so much. Everything. It meant Gard's safety, and this man's future, perhaps this man's life. She must be absolutely sure.

She was led along the line, staring at each one, until she reached the seventh man, who had a small scar on his nostril, and who was breathing very hard.

She stood still, in front of him.

Her hand raised.

"All right, Miss Smith," Parsons said, quietly. "You can talk to us afterwards. Take a close look at everyone."

Inside the office a few minutes afterwards, she said: "It's the man I stopped near! Number seven! I'm absolutely, absolutely sure."

"You know that you'll have to give evidence at his trial, don't you?"

"I can't help what I have to do. I'm absolutely *sure.*"

"Why did you wait so long before attacking Delancy?" Gideon asked Robson.

"I—I don't know," the man answered hesitantly. "It drove me crazy, I hardly knew what I was doing. I have spells like that, I . . ."

"You own a Ford Zephyr, black in colour," Gideon said. "Why did you drive it at Delancy with intent to kill him?"

Robson went very pale.

"Was it because you thought he had recognized you at the tube station?" demanded Gideon. "Or was it because you couldn't wait any longer to kill him?"

"It—it was an accident," muttered Robson.

"He's going to plead insanity, but the fact that he waited four years will probably convince the jury that he was sane enough to be patient—and didn't want to get caught," Lemaitre said to Gideon later.

That evening, when Delancy said good night to Emily outside the little Ealing house, it was more than ever difficult to part. Delancy made himself go at last, and Emily stood in the porch watching until he was out of sight.

Delancy turned the corner of the street where he lived, three quarters of an hour later. It was half past twelve, and practically every light was out, but there was one at his house. He was almost positive that his mother was waiting up for him. He steeled himself to unlock the door and go in.

"Is that you, Hildegard?" his mother called from the front room.

"Mum, it's all over," he said hurriedly. "There's nothing

else to worry about. They've caught the man—thanks to Emily. If it weren't for her, I might be dead by now."

"I know, dear. And of course I'm grateful. Very grateful. Now come along and have some nice warm soup. I'm sure you need it, after a long day."

He followed her, realizing then that he would have to gear himself for a fight, and now and again wondering if the best way would be to get married quickly, and cut out the waiting period. If they were married in a month, say, his mother would have to accept it. That might be the best way to handle the situation.

If Emily would agree . . .

A week later, Boman and Parsons received invitations to the Delancy-Smith wedding. The reception was to be held in a church hall in Ealing, not in Hounslow.

When Gideon heard of it, he remembered Chindini's precise voice, his remarkable control of the facts, and his confidence in Delancy. Delancy was heading for promotion and perhaps higher things than he expected.

The wedding invitations came after the biggest headache for London that week. Seven depots were on strike in protest against the arrests of the two inspectors. Among those to suffer was Peggy Blessington who sometimes took a taxi but more often walked when the bus route she needed was affected.

But there was a glorious compensation. Nearly every day, at some bus stop or other, George would be waiting in the Jaguar, to take her on her errands.

Her love for and trust in him strengthened every day.

Studying all the London Transport reports, Gideon came to the conclusion that Detective Sergeant King and Boman had taken the only possible course, but that there were some grounds for thinking that Ware and Dibben might be victims of a frame-up. There were gaps in the case against them, and the more he studied these the wider they seemed to get. Moreover, no one could yet trace anyone to whom they had sold stolen goods.

"As things stand," he said to Hobbs and Boman, "a good defence counsel could get these chaps off. Unless we can find out where they sold the goods, I doubt if we could make a charge of being in possession of stolen goods stick."

"That's what I told Corrington," Boman said, eagerly. "Do you know what he's going to do?"

Gideon waited.

"He's going to pay for the best defence counsel in England," Boman said. "He's a crafty so-and-so, George. Do you know what he's said in a statement to the garage? He says that if these arrests had been carried out by London Transport Police it would have created a very difficult situation, but as they were carried out by the Metropolitan Police, he believes that the Board should pay for the best counsel possible to help such old and faithful servants. Touch of genius, isn't it? I can almost hear them talking in the garages. I'm told that Willesden's going back tonight."

Corrington leaned back in an armchair at his home, that evening, with Moira sitting on the arm of it. The television news announcer glanced down at the script in front of him, and then looked up and said:

"Back to work at the seven London bus garages and the two Underground depots. That is the result of a ballot among the staff and crews concerned. According to Press Association reports the vote to return to work was almost unanimous. The two men charged with being in possession of stolen goods were remanded on bail, and are due for the second hearing next Tuesday."

"We're over this hump," said Corrington. "But it's going to be a tricky week-end. If things go wrong at the hearing on

Tuesday the men might come out again. There's a lot of sympathy for Dibben and Ware, and—" he moved across the lovely room, such a remarkable contrast to the crowded parlour of the Wares' house, where Ware himself was sitting dejectedly at that very moment. "It's going to be a tough week-end for Ware and Dibben and their families, too."

"Don't you think you've enough to worry about yourself?" Moira asked. "Try to relax for the week-end."

For the Gideons it was a fairly quiet week-end. Kate could tell how preoccupied George was, particularly about the Wares and the Dibbens. Twice he made an excuse to telephone the Division, and after the second call, he said:

"They're putting up a brave front, anyhow. The two families are living in each other's pockets."

"Hating the police?" Kate suggested.

"You bet they are!"

The Sabbath was also disturbed by a call from Ringall, to tell Gideon that he now knew beyond doubt that there was a large-scale smuggling of Irish whiskey into Wales, and that it should not be long before arrests were made. Soon afterwards Parsons telephoned to say that he had heard that there was a "secret" meeting of the Action Committees at which Higson and the two electrical technicians were present.

"It looks like being a late-night session too," Parsons reported. "Boman and I are checking the case against Dibben and Ware as if our own lives depended on it. Those two have got under my skin."

"I know what you mean," Gideon said.

Parsons and Boman were as uneasy as he, of course, and most of the day he was preoccupied with the London Transport case. Only once or twice did he give a fleeting thought to the Seaside Strangler.

* * *

For Peggy Blessington, Saturday was everything she had ever dreamed—everything, and more.

George was—wonderful. That was the only word she could think of. They went off in his Jaguar, and she had the thrill of a breathtaking drive along the M1 Motorway before he turned off for the winding country roads. Now and again he would glance at her, eagerly, and she sensed the great excitement in him, too; and desire. Her fears and her guilt were almost dead, she was so happy, so sure of her lover-to-be.

He slowed down along a road near the river, a winding one with a cottage here and there, some houseboats, and a few caravans drawn up close to the water. To her surprise, he pulled into a gateway of a small field which led down to the river. In a corner, shaded by a great oak tree, was a little blue caravan. He stopped the car a few yards away from it, his hand touched hers. He said:

"There's our little bit of heaven, my darling."

His voice quivered, and she could not speak, her lips were trembling so. For a fleeting, frightened moment, she felt that she could not go into the caravan, but as she stood on the grass outside, George moved and lifted her high, and carried her in.

He kissed her.

"Darling," he said, in a husky voice, "there's nothing to be afraid of. Absolutely nothing."

He was so gentle.

His hands were cool upon her flesh as he slid her clothes off, and it did not dawn on her how practised he must be. The bed was narrow, but firm. He caressed and kissed and quietened her trembling, and possessed her, so that she knew ecstasy.

Afterwards, in a dream world, they swam, and talked, and ate a little, walked along the river and through the woods, until towards dusk they returned to the caravan.

Could such ecstasy come back?

He loved to stroke her, and the soft, sensuous movement of his hands put her into a kind of trance, deeper than a dream. For a while she did not realize that the pressure of his hands and his body upon her was greater and more urgent. All gentleness fled. She felt herself responding to his urgency. Nothing had ever been so vital; passion took on the glory of a raging fire.

His hands were about her head, about her face, about her neck—holding, gripping, *hurting*.

Then she saw that his eyes were different; they seemed to be ablaze, they seemed to protrude.

Suddenly, in awful fear, the ecstasy died, and she began to struggle.

George Cope buried the body in the river bank, instead of the golden sands of the seashore. Then he cleaned the caravan of his prints, confident that it would never be traced to him, for he had rented it by mail, sending a money order in payment and giving a false name.

On the Tuesday morning, at the East London Magistrate's Court, one of the biggest crowds ever gathered was assembled for the second hearing of the Ware-Dibben case. Newspapermen, neighbours, sightseers, busmen, tubemen, and a positive swarm of Ware relatives, including the babies in arms, were outside the court. Very few could get inside.

Corrington was there.

Gideon was present, at Boman's urgent request, although Christie and King were to be the witnesses for the prosecution. Gideon did not think he had ever seen a more pathetic sight than Ware, standing stiffly in the dock, and Dibben glaring about him deviantly. Mrs. Dibben was in court, but Mrs. Ware was at home in a state of collapse.

The evidence was given exactly as Gideon knew it would be, following the plea of Not Guilty. He had never been at a hearing before when he so wanted a verdict adverse to him, but here were the facts, speaking for themselves. The stolen goods were on a bench, in court. The two lighters were marked Exhibit A, and the two pound notes Exhibit B. The cold facts seemed to condemn the two men where they stood.

Counsel rose, at the magistrate's invitation. He was a man whom Gideon knew well, who was brilliant in the Assizes, and who had not pleaded in a Magistrate's Court for many years. He was middle-aged, greying, resonant, and yet quiet-voiced. He dwelt first upon the character of these two men, and the service they had given to London's Transport. He told of the history of the Museum, of their devotion, their love of London's buses and trains.

Would such men betray the trust in themselves as well as in the cause they served? Was it conceivable?

Corrington was watching intently. Boman, sitting next to Gideon, leaned closer and said:

"They haven't found anything, George. He's trying the emotional line, but it won't get 'em off. God knows what will happen now."

The magistrate's clerk glowered at Boman.

Was it even conceivable that two such men . . . and was there a scrap of evidence that they had ever sold stolen goods . . . or in fact had known where the goods were?

"They took mostly money," Boman whispered. "Hard cash."

Gideon nodded.

A door leading from the cells opened, a policeman glanced round, saw Gideon, and while the counsel was still pleading that lost cause, came to Gideon and thrust a message into his hands. Gideon opened it, and read:

> "New witness on the way. Suggest postpone for an hour. Chap says he knows who took the stuff and put it in the Museum to frame the pair.
>
> Lem."

Gideon leaned forward, the magistrate frowned, his clerk stood up to rebuke, but by then the message had reached Christie. There was a mild sensation when he asked for a two hours' postponement.

Gideon waited until the case was adjourned, hurried out, and went to the nearest telephone.

"Can't tell you any more, George, except that this chap says that the thieves were two electrical maintenance men," Lemaitre said. "The amazing thing is, the witness is one of the Action Committee. The man Higson. He says that these chaps used to help at the Museum sometimes, so they knew where to hide the stuff. They slipped the money and the lighters in Dibben's and Ware's pockets to clinch the case."

What Lemaitre and Gideon would never know was that on that late Sunday session, the Action Committees had condemned the methods used to create the conditions for a strike, and confirmed the rule that everything they did must be within the law. Two of their members were to be sacrificed to that purpose.

Gideon stood in an office above the court, watching the crowd outside holding up the traffic, as Ware and Dibben were chaired shoulder high, and the mob kept cheering them, the Ware family seemed to go mad with delight, and Mrs. Dibben, head held high and proudly, hurried to tell Mrs. Ware that everything was all right, everything was over.

Gideon went to Christie's office, and had a word with Detective Sergeant King. He had a feeling that the man would always be aggressive and sometimes hasty, but he had given his evidence well, and certainly knew his job. In this tough district, there was room for aggression.

"Glad to know you're joining the inspectors," Gideon said. "Congratulations."

King's delight suggested beyond reasonable doubt that he was first and last a policeman.

Gideon went back to his office, found Lemaitre busy, but

ready to sit back and talk. *Who would believe it of Higson?* The important thing was, though, that it had worked out all right, the strike was off for good.

Gideon was non-committal.

Then Parsons came in. He was very sleek, very smooth, and even smug, rubbing his hands together as he stood in front of Gideon's desk.

"You look as if you're back on your Soho beat, and liking it," Gideon remarked.

"Well, I'm not," said Parsons. "Have you seen the report in from Stratford-on-Avon?"

"It's under the pile on your desk," Lemaitre called across. Gideon looked for the file.

"Tell me all about it," he invited.

"I don't like the look of it," said Parsons. "A girl's been found dead near the River Avon, between Stratford and Henley-in-Arden. This girl's fair-haired, aged about nineteen, very like the Seaside Strangler's victims. She was killed sometime over the week-end, and buried in the mud. There's a queer thing, George—she was a messenger for an insurance company, and travelled around London a lot by bus. I'd like to take over before Ringall gets back from Llandudno, and I'd like another go at all the conductors on the routes she travelled by. I'd put up a photograph of that girl in all the London bus depots, too. I'd like—"

"All right," said Gideon. "Handle it right away, but keep me in touch."

"See you," said Parsons, and hurried out.

The next day, when the photograph was pinned to the notice board of his depot, Conductor Paddy O'Neil stared at it, and felt as if something had been taken out of his life.

All members of bus crews are asked to give the police all possible assistance in this matter, read the caption.

"Be sure I will," said Paddy O'Neil, aloud. "Be certain, certain positive I will."

The news of the murder of Peggy Blessington, the thought that if they had caught the Seaside Strangler earlier the girl would still be alive, depressed Gideon. He was still glum when he left the office, about six o'clock that evening, and looked down in the mouth when he reached home. Kate opened the front door, as she always did if she had any news for him. His mood brightened when he saw her.

He kissed her lightly on the cheek.

"I'm glad you're home early, dear," she said as they went along to the kitchen, where a casserole was sizzling and appetizing. "You probably think I was wrong, but I took a chance and called on Mrs. Hobbs this afternoon. She's *quite* lovely, it's a tragic thing. But she's delightful, too. And we're going along to coffee, after supper—about eight o'clock. You don't think Alec Hobbs will mind, do you?"

"No, he won't mind," said Gideon, feeling himself again. "It's just right, Kate, It's fine."